SWEET PEA

BURNING SAINTS MC BOOK #4

JACK DAVENPORT

2nd Edition 2020 Jack Davenport
Copyright © 2019, 2020-2022 Trixie Publishing, Inc.
All rights reserved.
Published in the United States

Sweet Pea is a work of fiction. Names, characters, places, and incidents are the products of the author's imagination and are used fictitiously. Any resemblance to actual events, locales, or persons, living or dead, is entirely coincidental.

Cover Art
Jack Davenport

Cover Model
Joe Adams

TRIXIE
PUBLISHING
ISBN: 9798619617917

Oh, good gravy, this book is good. And I'm not just saying that because he does other amazing things with his fingers!

~ **Piper Davenport, Contemporary Romance Author**

Liz Kelly
Your insights are amazing and always spot on. Thank you!

Piper
I couldn't do any of this without you. Literally, my fingers would fall off and I'd be a vegetable.

Brandy G.
Thank you for the million reads and your attention to detail!!! You're amazing.

Gail G.
You're a rock star! Thank you for all your help!

Mary H.
Thank you! You're an angel!

For Joe
Thanks for wearing a helmet, buddy.

ONE

BURNING SAINTS

Sweet Pea

"**L**ADIES AND GENTLEMEN of the jury, before this trial concludes, I would like to thank you all once again for your service to this court. I know the witness testimony was difficult to listen to and appreciate the difficult task you were all asked to perform."

Judge Reynolds addressed the jury in a sensitive tone, rarely heard from behind his bench. The trial had been hell on everyone in the courtroom and the tension was at an all-time high as we were now moments away from hearing the final verdict.

"Madam Foreperson, has the jury reached a unanimous decision?"

The foreperson rose to her feet, the verdict held in her trembling hand. "Yes, your Honor, we have."

My pulse quickened and I felt beads of sweat form on my brow.

"The defendant will now rise for the reading of the verdict in the case of the State of Oregon vs. John Knight," Judge Reynolds' baritone voice boomed out. Disgraced evangelical pastor, John Knight, stood, flanked by his lawyers. His typical douchebag uniform of bedazzled jeans and Ed Hardy shirt was replaced with a drab grey suit and tie. One more disguise to make him look like a respectable minister and not the predatory monster he was. Not that it mattered. After what the jury heard, there was no way this guy would ever see daylight again, let alone the pulpit of his hipster church.

As soon as he was on his feet, Knight attempted to charm the jury one last time, making eye contact with each member. His lips pressed into a half-smile of fake humility, mouthing the words, "Bless you."

"Please direct your attention to the bench, Mr. Knight," Judge Reynolds said sternly, and Knight did as he was told.

"Before I instruct the foreperson to read the verdict, I would like to take a few moments to address you personally."

The room was so quiet I thought the person next to me would be able to hear my heart thumping inside my chest. I was normally cool as a cucumber, but this trial had me crawling out of my skin with nerves. Like everyone else in the room, I wanted it to be over and for Knight to pay.

Judge Reynolds continued, "Mr. Knight, it is the firm belief of this court that you willingly and knowingly gained the trust of the good people of this community, and then, not only abused that trust, but the children of the very people who gave it to you. I believe you are an evil man in shepherd's clothing. A man that used his position of authority for financial gain and to sexually abuse children."

Every muscle in my body tightened. I wanted to leap over the divider that separated us and choke the life out of that piece of shit myself. I wasn't a fan of John Knight when he was just a two-bit local televangelist wannabe, but now I wanted him erased from the planet. I'd been obsessed with his case since the news of his arrest, and once the trial started, any time the club didn't need me, I was here in this courthouse. Now, I was finally going to see this bastard pay for his sins.

The judge continued, "If it were up to me, you'd never see the outside of a prison cell. However, in this case, it's up to the jury and I will have to trust them and the judicial system." Judge Reynolds turned to the foreperson. "Madam Foreperson, in the case of the State of Oregon vs. John Knight, how do you find the defendant, John Knight, on the first count of sexual assault on a minor?"

I've heard the term tunnel vision all my life but had never experienced it myself. What I experienced next was more like pinpoint vision. My field of vision was completely blacked out, except for a very narrow point of focus. The only thing I could see was the foreperson's mouth. Her cheap, drug store lipstick stained mouth forming the words, "Not guilty."

I saw and heard nothing for the next few minutes. Fugue states were not exactly uncommon for me during times of extreme stress. I'd "lost time" before, but it had been years since the last episode.

Once fully lucid again, I'd come to find the jury found Knight *not* guilty on all three charges, including sexual assault of a minor, as well as the lesser charges against him. In short, John Knight was about to leave the courtroom a free man.

Later, when asked, the members of the jury said they just couldn't believe that a man that was so clearly "used by God" and "filled with the Holy Spirt," could willingly harm a child. Despite the evidence and testimony from Elsie Miller herself, these people could not wrap their minds around this kind of evil.

I understood it all too well.

* * *

Callie

"Not guilty."

After she read the verdict on the final count, the foreperson folded the verdict sheet and looked at Judge Reynolds who sat silently. If this had been any other courtroom, pandemonium would have surely broken out by now, but the judge had already made it perfectly clear that he would not tolerate any outbursts in his courtroom. He'd proven that twice on the first day of trial by removing two family members and a reporter for what he called inappropriate behavior.

"It is with great regret that I must declare this trial concluded. Mr. Knight, you are free to go," Judge Reynolds said, and hastily banged his gavel before quickly exiting through the side door that led to his chambers.

I'd worked in his courtroom enough times to know when he was unhappy, but I'm not sure I'd ever seen him stunned before. Not that I could blame him. This was, by far, the biggest miscarriage of justice I'd ever witnessed, let alone been a part of. I turned and made eye contact with my client, Elsie, and her mother, Rita. I tried to mouth the words, "I'm sorry," but my face betrayed me, choosing instead to convulse as I burst into tears.

"Callie? Are you okay?" Rob asked.

I heard him clearly, but responded with, "What?" I didn't know what else to say at that moment. I suppose I could have asked, "What the hell just happened?" or better yet, screamed, "What the actual fuck?" at the top of my lungs. Better still, I should have grabbed the fore-person and shook her silly. How could the jury have possibly come back with not guilty on all charges? I'll admit that my confidence wasn't at an all-time-high when it came to the third count, but *not guilty*? I knew it was a mistake to rush to trial, and I sure as hell would have handled jury selection entirely differently if I had been the lead prosecutor.

"Let's get out of here," Rob said and gently guided me through the sea of audience members and media. Rob Glass and I had both started at the DA's office around the same time and had worked together closely ever since. We made an excellent team and had assisted each other on several successful cases. This was not only our first loss, but by far, our most important and personal case.

"We have to talk to the Millers," I said in a panic.

"We will, Callie. Let's get you some air first," Rob said.

This case had consumed our lives for the past sixteen months, all leading up to a trial we thought would be a slam dunk. And it was. Our team had worked their fingers to the bone and our witness testimonies were as compelling as they come.

Our witnesses.

I began to openly sob as that thought washed over me. Our witnesses were a family who'd been ripped to shreds by a monster. A monster that was now free to prowl their neighborhoods again despite their bravery on the stand. I could not believe that we, the legal system and me personally, had let these children down.

Gregg Sterling, the lead prosecutor and the DA's golden boy, met Rob and me as we passed. "I'm so sorry. I know you both put a lot of hours into this case. This was a tough loss for all of us."

"Screw us!" I snapped. "This was a loss for Elsie. Not to mention, the children like her who haven't come forward yet. Or worse, the ones he's free to target now." I'd always been able to look past the fact that I didn't like Gregg on a personal level, but now that he'd blown the trial, I was outright hostile. "He's going to do this again, Gregg."

"Even though Knight walked, what kind of parent would let their kids near him now?" Gregg asked, flippantly.

"The kind that just voted him not guilty, Gregg. Were you asleep while the verdict was read?"

"Careful, Ms. Ames," Gregg warned.

"The truth is, you're so focused on becoming the next DA, you rushed through jury selection. I warned you about at least four of those jurors and you ignored me each time," I replied.

"What did you just say to me?"

"Oh, you heard me," I snapped. "Look at what just happened. The jury heard from the kids themselves and still let Knight walk. There are a lot of people out in the world who trust the church more than they trust their own eyes, ears, and guts. You overestimated your ability to select a jury and underestimated Knight's ability to work them."

"So, this was *my* fault?" Gregg asked.

"Getting justice for Elsie was our responsibility. The fact that you don't feel we failed her speaks volumes,

Gregg. Now, if you'll excuse me, I'd like to go try and help comfort the families if I can."

Rob and I continued our push through the crush of people into the hallway, which was now as crowded as the courtroom itself. Using our key cards, we gained access to the secured rear exit and made our way outside. I headed for the courthouse steps, but Rob stopped me.

"You sure you want to head right back into all that chaos? Maybe you should take a beat."

"I can't, Rob. I need to talk to the Millers. I need to explain to them how sorry I am that we failed."

"You did everything you could have, Callie. This wasn't your failure."

"Come on," I said, ignoring his words. I knew he was only trying to make me feel better, but there was no way in hell I wasn't going to take this personally. The initial shock of the loss already transitioning to rage within the pit of my stomach. A rage that would only be quelled by justice. Although, right now I'd take Knight's blood as a substitute.

"You should have been lead counsel on this case, Callie. Everyone knows it, including Sterling," Rob said.

"It's too late now," I said. "We failed."

"Maybe someday Knight will get what he deserves," Rob said.

"Maybe," I replied.

As we reached the front of the courthouse, I was horrified to see John Knight standing at the top of the stairs, surrounded by reporters and spectators. It was bad enough he was free, but true to his twisted nature, Knight was using this moment as an opportunity to preach.

"It's truly a blessing to know that God's protective

hand has been on me during this trying ordeal," I heard Knight say as we approached.

With every word he spoke, my anger level rose.

"I can only pray God's mercy and healing upon young Elsie Miller and her family," Knight continued, and I started toward him.

Rob gently but firmly grabbed my elbow, pulling me to him. "Callie, don't," was all he said, and as much as I didn't want to listen to him, I did.

I knew Rob was looking out for me and my career, and as much as I didn't give a rat's ass about my job at the moment, bludgeoning a member of the clergy on the courthouse steps in front of a gaggle of reporters wasn't a great plan.

It was only after Knight said the following that my rage turned to something darker. Something that made my own personal wheels of justice begin to turn in the opposite direction.

"Before I go and spend some much-needed time with family, I'd like to address the Miller family, if you are out there. I'd like to say that I forgive you. I forgive you with all of my heart for your misguided character assassination attempt on me and I pray for justice for whoever harmed your daughter."

"We need to find Elsie, right now," I said to Rob, hoping and praying the Millers weren't hearing any of this. "You look over there," I said motioning to the east side of the building, "and I'll check the other side."

I scanned the crowd until I saw the Millers on the opposite side of the steps. Far from the sound of John Knight's voice for the moment, but not far enough from him for my liking. I would have preferred they be separated by thick concrete walls and iron bars.

Sweet Pea

I had to hit someone in the face. Right fucking now.

"Stay in a single file line! Have your claim tickets ready!" A faceless government employee called out from somewhere in the crowded hallway. The courthouse had a strict no cellphone policy and the high-profile nature of this case meant the phone return line for court observers was longer than usual. Once I'd reached the front of the line, I turned in my ticket, and powered my phone up the instant it was back in my hands. I called our club's Sergeant at Arms and luckily, Clutch picked up right away.

"What's up, Pea?" Clutch shouted. I could tell from the background noise that he was at his gym.

"You got anyone there lookin' to spar?"

"You want me to set you up a training schedule?" he asked.

Our club had a stake in several businesses and Clutch Combat Sports was one of them. It had been a few months since I'd been in the ring, but today I needed some place to put my rage.

"No, I mean right now. As in, right fuckin' now."

"Oh, shit. The pastor didn't walk, did he?" Clutch asked.

"You got someone I can spar with or not?" I asked, unable to hide my anger.

"Not if you're in a shitty mood! Especially not your giant Viking ass. It's hard enough for me to find guys your height, let alone anywhere near your size. Plus, I don't have time to visit people in the fucking hospital right now, Sweet Pea."

"I'll go half power, I swear."

"Who do you swear to exactly, religiously speaking?

Does Odin take your calls directly?"

"Come on, Clutch."

"Sorry, man. I can't trust your lightning bolt throwin' motherfucking ass. Come on down, I'll tape you up really good and put you on the heavy bag until you can't lift your arms anymore, but that's it."

"Not good enough. I gotta make someone pay."

"That's exactly why I'm *not* gonna put you in the ring right now," he replied.

I exited the building and hit the top of the courthouse steps. I was making my way through the swirling chaos of humanity when I spotted Callie Ames from the prosecution team. I'd had a hard time keeping my eyes off her the entire trial. In fact, I wondered if I would have made it to court quite so many times had she not been there. I'd seen her at previous family court hearings and was always struck by her beauty. Callie was tall, blonde and wore everything as if it was tailor made for her.

She was talking with the Miller family, and I was surprised and moved to see her visibly crying with the families over the obvious injustice that had been committed against them. In court, Callie Ames was completely composed. She came across as highly professional, but without seeming cold. She was striking and elegant. More like a movie star cast as a lawyer than someone you'd expect to be the real thing. I'd been inside this courtroom more times than I could count, had seen my fair share of lawyers, and most of them looked more like Paul Giamatti than Blake Lively.

"Alright," I said, half-heartedly returning my attention to Clutch. "Maybe, I'll come by."

"Don't do anything stupid, Pea. The last thing we need right now is you socking some jerk in the mouth over a parking space just because you're all twisted up about this pervert going free."

"Yeah."

"I mean it," Clutch said, clearly speaking to me as a superior. "The stitches on your Road Captain's patch are still clean and the club doesn't need any extra heat right now."

"You think I don't fuckin' know that?" I shot back.

"Just make sure you remember it."

I couldn't take my eyes off Callie, who was down on one knee, speaking with her young client, Elsie Miller. She was showing a display of strength for the little girl, but I could see the pain in her eyes as she comforted her.

"You hear me, man?" Clutch asked

"Yeah," I replied, having barely processed the last thing he'd said. My gaze was fixed on Callie and she was beginning to put a real damper on my rage. In fact, the more I stared at her the more my anger dissolved into the ether.

Callie glanced up at me for only a nanosecond before returning to the little girl and giving her a hug as the family said their goodbyes.

"I'll call you back, Clutch," I said and hung up before giving him the chance to reply, shocked to see Callie Ames walking straight toward me. We made eye contact and I froze, shocked that she was approaching. I thought about what, if anything I should say, when she beat me to the punch.

"Hello, Mr. Kimble."

Sweet Pea

Two

ER GREETING MADE my blood run cold. "How the fuck do you know my name?" I growled. To say I was stunned would be putting it lightly.

"Odd question for a guy who walks around wearing a name tag." Callie grinned and pointed to the patch on my kutte. "I'm Callie—"

"I know who you are. You called me Mr. Kimble. How did you know my… birth name?" I asked with equal amount intrigue and annoyance.

"I'm resourceful," she replied nonchalantly.

"Okay, but…"

"I couldn't help but notice you've been staring at me."

"I didn't mean to stare, I was just...I saw you with Elsie Miller and I just..."

"Yes?" Callie prodded. Her tone remained sweet, but I felt like I was on the stand.

"I thought you were great during the trial and I'm sorry you lost the case." Callie's expression softened and I continued, "I appreciate you being there for that little girl and her family. At least...for trying anyway."

Callie cleared her throat. "Thank you, Mr. Kimble. I must admit, this was sweet of you and unexpected."

"Yeah, again about the Kimble thing," I said, looking around. "How exactly do you know who I am?"

"Giant bikers tend to stand out in places like courthouses," she replied.

"That doesn't explain how you know my real name."

"Lawyers have access to legal documents, and name change requests are easily accessible."

"Still not an explanation," I said, now more annoyed than intrigued.

"Let's just say I tend to get curious about outlaw bikers who may or may not be stalking me."

"Stalking you? I've never stalked anyone in my life," I protested.

"Then why are you here at the courthouse?"

"I'm not the only member of the public here today. I have an interest in this case. That's all."

"What about the eight cases before this one?"

"Have I done something wrong?" I asked.

"Please answer the question. Why does an outlaw biker spend so much time in a courthouse?"

"Look, I'm not stalking anyone, okay? Lawyers or otherwise," I said, defensively. "I haven't done jack shit and didn't come here to be put on trial myself."

Callie's expression softened and her shoulders dropped. "You're right. I'm sorry, it's been a very long, very bad day. You're being sweet and I'm being rude. I owe you an apology."

"You don't owe me shit," I said. "After what you just went through. Hell, after what that family just went through... don't even worry about me."

Callie paused and studied my face.

"You're not at all what I expected," she said softly.

"Expected? What do you mean?"

"I have something I want to show you," Callie said, sidestepping my question.

"What could you possibly have for me?"

I could think of a few things.

"How about you let me buy you a cup of coffee tomorrow and I'll bring it to you?" Callie asked.

"I have church tomorrow and I hate coffee, but I know a place we can get a beer right now. You look like you could use a drink."

"Oh, my God, I'm probably wrecked," she said, wiping her eyes.

"No, that's not what I meant, you look fucking amazing," I blurted out, causing Callie to blush instantly.

A man I recognized as Callie's co-council emerged from the crowd and approached us. He placed his hand on Callie's arm and the moment he touched her, I wanted to go full-on Wookie on the guy. His action shouldn't have elicited any type of emotional response from me, let alone wanting to remove his arm from its socket, but it did.

"Everything okay, Callie?" he asked in what I think was meant to be a protective tone. He came off sounding more like a wolf pup practicing its howl for the first time.

"I'm great, Rob, thanks," Callie said sweetly to him, who then turned to me.

"Rob Glass," he said, extending his hand, which I left unshaken.

"Mr. Kimble was just thanking our office for our work on the case." Callie turned to me.

"It's Sweet Pea," I replied. "And I wasn't thanking your office, I was thanking you."

"No offense taken," Rob said with a nervous laugh.

My focus remained entirely on Callie. "So, about that drink?" I asked.

"Drink?" Rob asked.

Callie smiled, and without breaking eye contact, reached into the side pocket of her leather satchel and produced a business card which she handed to me. "Text me at this number with the location and I'll meet you there at eight o'clock." she said.

"Sounds perfect," I said with a smile and a nod, and walked away.

* * *

Callie

"What the hell was that all about?" Rob asked.

"I honestly have no idea," I replied, equally as stunned, but trying to keep my composure.

"Why did he come over here?"

"Rob, I don't know. I was standing here, talking with the Millers, and he just strolled on over like he didn't have a care in the world," I lied. He didn't need to know it was me who approached Sweet Pea.

Rob leaned in and whispered, "Does he know about the file? And what was that about meeting you for a drink?"

"I told you, I don't know. It all happened so fast.

"Callie, the Burning Saints are stone cold criminals and we have no idea what this Sweet Pea guy has planned for you."

I could tell Rob was genuinely concerned, and I appreciated that, but I also sensed a desire to protect me that felt more romantic than friendly. As much as I liked and respected Rob I never viewed him as anything more than a friend. There were times, however, when I feared he wanted more from our relationship. Admittedly, I was never great about picking up on romantic social cues, spending most of my high school and college days studying rather than mastering the art of dating as many of my friends seemed to do.

"I'd never go anywhere I didn't feel safe. Besides, wherever we're meeting is going to be a public place, so what's he going to do? Whack me in the middle of some Italian eatery?"

"You're making mob jokes, but you're not too far off, Callie. You know the violence these clubs are capable of. Besides, after what you just went through, do you really think that you're in shape enough emotionally to meet a biker for drinks?"

"I think I can take care of myself and my *emotions* just fine, thank you," I snapped.

"Come on Callie. That's not what I meant, and you know it."

I did and he was probably right, not that it would stop me from meeting with Kimble. Rob didn't need to know the real reason I was meeting with Kimble. In fact, the less he knew the better. For his sake.

"All I'm saying," Rob continued, "is that you've been through a lot over the course of this trial and we're all pretty wrecked over what just went down in there. I just want to make sure you're making clear-headed decisions when it comes to your safety and well-being."

Rob meant well and was right. I was crispy around the edges and the last thing I should be doing was exactly what I was about to do.

"As soon as Kimble texts me with the location, I'll text you. Okay?"

"Don't be a hero, Callie. If you feel unsafe at any time, you get the hell out of there and call the police."

"I will," I replied but Rob looked unconvinced, so I held up my right hand. "I swear."

"Do you need a lift home?" Rob asked.

"That's super sweet, but no thank you. I'm going to head back to the office before meeting Kimble. I'll just get an Uber," I said pulling out my phone.

"You're going back to the office? Don't you ever take a break?"

"I need to grab something from the office before I meet with him. I can get changed there."

"Of course, you have a spare change of clothes at the office."

"Spare clothes are what you keep in your bottom drawer, Rob. I have a portable dressing station. I don't fuck around," I said with a smile.

"No, I suppose you don't," he replied before turning and heading for the parking garage.

THREE

BURNING SAINTS

Sweet Pea

I SAT ON my bike and stared at Callie Ames's business card, trying to make sense of what the fuck had just happened. My identity wasn't exactly a state secret, but given my personal family history, it wasn't like I was public about it either. Apart from my brother, Ropes, my family was dead as fucking doornails to me. The same went for the Kimble name. Sweet Pea was all anyone had ever called me since arriving in Portland over ten years ago. Cutter had given me the name before I was even a prospect.

Clutch answered my call right away. "You change your mind about the heavy bag?"

"What? No, I'm cool. Listen," I continued. "Something interesting just happened, but I don't wanna say anything more over the phone. Can you meet me at Sally Anne's in twenty minutes?"

"I'll change and meet you there," Clutch said, and hung up.

I fired up my bike and headed for Sally Anne's. The plan was to meet with Clutch and fill him in on my conversation with Callie before she and I met for drinks. I figured if I was on some lawyer's radar, that meant heat on the club which was the last thing we needed right now. This could also be nothing, but since I wasn't sure what was what yet, I figured I'd run it by Clutch before bothering Minus. God knows he had enough on his plate right now.

Our club was on the verge of a major turf war with the Gresham Spiders, who were looking to expand the size of their web. The Spiders were as dangerous as clubs came, and they both outgunned and outnumbered us. Minus had already gathered the support of just about every other local MC in hopes that the Spiders would back off, but we had no idea how they'd respond to our show of force. After going to the joint the Spiders' President, Char, poached my old Road Captain, Wolf, to act as the Spiders' President while he's locked up. The whole situation was as powder keg in a fucking match factory.

I was so preoccupied with my thoughts that I'd ridden to Sally Anne's completely on autopilot. It was the second time today I'd totally blanked out. First in the courtroom after Knight's verdict was read and now during my ride. I made a mental note of the date and promised myself I'd talk to Ropes about it as soon as possible.

"Hey there, Sweetie Peaty," Sally Anne's familiar

rasp sang out as soon as I entered the bar.

"How you doin', gorgeous?" I replied with a smile.

"Still waitin' for you to make an honest woman outta me," Sally Anne said as she pulled the tap handle of my favorite local brew.

There were only a few patrons in the place, and currently no other Saints were present, but it was still early.

"You greet me with a beer like that every time I come through the door and I just might change my mind about marriage," I said.

Sally Anne grinned wickedly. "Honey, I'd greet you with a hell of a lot more than a beer every night if we were hitched."

"What makes you think I could keep up with you?" I asked, playfully.

"Who says I think you could? I'd chop you down like a big ol' oak tree, baby."

I laughed and took a pull from my beer just as Clutch walked up to the bar.

"What's going on?" Clutch asked, wasting no time on pleasantries.

"Let's go sit down," I said motioning to the club's private table as Sally Anne handed him a tall glass filled with ice and clear liquid. "Vodka and soda?" I asked, surprised at Clutch's drink of choice.

"Worse," he replied. "Just fucking soda."

"You in training?"

"No, but the Kid is. I have to stay in shape just to keep with up, let alone train him."

"He just won his first big fight. Isn't it time to relax a little?"

He laughed. "You try telling him that. He's a machine. Besides, now that I've got the wife and kids, I'm trying drink less and eat better."

"Your old lady's got you on a shot leash, huh?" I

razzed.

"No, man. It's not like that. I just want to be around for them is all. It's kinda hard to explain, but starting a family made me *want* to change certain things about myself."

"That sounds goddamned awful," I said.

"Don't let the Doc here you say that, she'll try and set you up with one of her friends just to try and break you."

"It'll *never* be me standing up in front of everyone, wearing a fucking monkey suit."

Clutch laughed. "I guess one hopeless romantic is enough for the family, huh?"

Clutch wasn't Cupid's only recent victim within the Burning Saints' clubhouse. My brother, Ropes, had not only recently fallen in love but had also started a career as a romance novelist of all fucking things. I could barely believe it. A hardcore biker writing romance books. I knew my brother more than I knew myself sometimes and even I didn't see that one coming.

"Look, man. I'm happy for you and your whole family."

"Good, because you'd have to fake it at Alejandro's victory party otherwise. You're gonna be there, right?"

"Of course, but I'd better not be walking into some sort of honey trap you and Eldie have set up."

"Jesus, Pea. How afraid of commitment are you?"

"It's not like that. I've just never seen myself settling down with one woman."

"You been thinking of getting some of those sister wives instead?"

"You know what I mean. The whole buying a big house and starting a family thing. None of that shit was ever on my radar. Now, every time I turn around, another brother is going off and getting civilized."

"You make it sound like we've all moved to the suburbs and got suit and tie jobs at Gunnach Industries or something."

"It kinda fuckin' feels like that sometimes," I said.

"What's the matter? Not enough people trying to kill us right now for your taste?" Clutch snapped, his tone turning serious.

"That's not what I meant," I replied.

"Be careful. Getting your back up about the domestication of the club is gonna remind some of the brothers of your old mentor. Let's not forget the reason you're wearing his patch in the first place."

"Like I don't know?" I fired back. "I may be wearing Wolf's old patch, but that doesn't mean I'm anything fucking like him."

"I never said you were, Pea." Clutch's scowl disappeared and his tone softened. "All I'm saying is that change is inevitable. We knew the club would change when Cutter died, and even more so when Minus became the prez. Shit man, my life has changed more than anyone else's in the club. Except maybe for your brother, D.W. Foxblood, Jr."

I laughed at his good-natured dig at Ropes and appreciated his attempt to break the tension. Something the Burning Saints didn't need any more of right now. Despite love being in the air, the past year or so had also been filled with a shit ton of violence and chaos, and there would be even more to come should Wolf and the Spiders decide to continue with their expansion into Portland.

"I'm sure you didn't call me here just to talk about marriage and boxing so, what's up?" Clutch asked.

"Could be nothing, but I figured I'd best be safe and let you know."

"Alright," Clutch said, taking a sip of his club soda.

"So, I was at the courthouse—"

"You still do that shit? Appear in court when you don't fuckin' have to?" Clutch asked. "I swear to God, there's something wrong with you, Pea."

"Yeah, well. While I was there, a lawyer kind of noticed me," I said, as casually as possible, suddenly wishing we could go back to talking about wedding planning. "A family lawyer who works in the DA's office."

Clutch shrugged. "A lawyer saw you at the courthouse, big deal."

I scratched the back of my neck. "It's a little more complicated than that."

Clutch's face fell. "For the love of Elvis, what the fuck have you done?"

"Nothing, I swear, just attended a few court hearings now and again. When the club didn't need me, and I guess—"

"Haven't Ropes and I both told you to be careful? That hanging out there was gonna make someone suspicious?" Clutch asked, unable or unwilling to hide the irritation in his voice.

"Yeah, but—"

"And now, some lawyer can't help but ask himself why a big ass biker is constantly roaming the halls of the courthouse. Right?"

"Something like that. Yeah, I guess."

"So, what's he know about the club?"

"I'll know more in a couple hours."

"Why's that exactly?"

"Because she's meeting me here later for a drink."

"She?"

"It's not like that," I said. "The whole thing was her damned idea."

"And you had to say yes?"

"She said she has something for me," I replied.

"I'll bet she does." Clutch paused before letting out a slow, low groan. "Oh, shit. She's hot, isn't she?"

"Her looks have nothing to do with this, and like I said, she asked me."

Clutch threw his hands in the air. "I knew it! She's fucking hot."

I leaned in and whispered, "She knew my real name."

"You'd better hope that's all she knows."

"Why do you think I wanted to tell you about this right away?"

Clutch relaxed his posture. "You're right. You did the right thing. I'm gonna hold off from saying anything to the prez until you report back to me, but I want to know what you know A.S.A. fucking P., you understand?"

"I will."

"And please do your best not to fuck her, would ya? Whatever mess you've gotten yourself into is only gonna get worse if you get your dick involved."

"Weren't you the one that was just telling me to find a nice girl and think about settling down?"

"A nice girl, Pea, not a fucking lawyer."

Clutch slammed down the rest of his club soda and waved goodbye to Sally Anne before leaving me alone with my thoughts.

* * *

Callie

As promised, I texted Rob with the meeting place as soon as Kimble had texted me. He wanted to meet at a local biker bar called Sally Anne's, which wasn't too much of a surprise given the Burning Saints owned the place. Rob replied immediately.

Rob: *I don't like it.*
Me: *It's a public place.*
Rob: *It's their turf.*
Me: *It's a bar with exit doors.*
Rob: *Doors have locks.*
Me: *I promise I'll leave if anything feels sketchy.*
Rob: *I'm on the record as saying this a bad idea, right?*
Me: *Noted.*

Now that Rob was in the loop, I could finish getting ready. I plugged in my curling iron and thumbed through the Kimble file while it heated up. I'd become a pro at dressing between hearings, depositions, and countless meetings. I found I was wasting precious time running back and forth to my apartment to get changed, so I turned almost half of my tiny office into a makeshift wardrobe. Ruby didn't require too much attention and was about as self-sufficient as a pet could be, but I was going to need to feed her soon. I made a mental note to stop by the pet store this weekend.

My phone buzzed again, and I huffed in annoyance. I was ready to put Rob on my Do Not Disturb list but was surprised to see it was another text from Sweet Pea.

Park in the back next to the bikes when you get here. No one will mess with your car.

I couldn't decide if his text made me feel more, or less, safe. I continued to dress knowing damned well that I was meeting him either way. I'd made up my mind the moment he'd asked, and if there was one thing that was true about me, it was that once my mind was made up, there was no changing it. Growing up, my dad used to say I was "as stubborn as a Baptist mule," but I didn't see myself that way. I was decisive, that's all. I was more than willing to change my mind, I just rarely did.

I texted back. *Taking an Uber. See you soon.*

I figured if he was planning on sending me to the depths of the Columbia River, he should know that my ride to Sally Anne's was documented and time stamped. Once I'd finished getting ready, I headed downstairs to wait for my ride.

"Good evening Miss Ames," Jerry, the evening security guard said as I passed him.

"Hi, Jerry. How are Yolanda and the girls?" I asked.

"Keesha is bugging us about her driver's permit every fifteen minutes and Tallah is obsessed with something called K-Pop."

"Oooh, that's rough."

"I'm in a house full of women who control the stereo, the TV, and what goes inside the refrigerator. Every one of them thinks I'm an idiot, and to make matters worse, they speak in some sort of female code that I don't understand."

I laughed. "How do you get through it all?"

He chuckled. "I'm here, working nights."

"Probably much quieter," I said.

"And safer." Jerry smiled wide. "I may be an idiot, but I'm not dumb."

My car arrived and my mind raced as we drove to Sally Anne's. I was starting to think Rob was right. Maybe I should have taken a beat to better process my feelings about the Knight case, but I was afraid if I did that, I'd talk myself out of what I was about to do. Even if the plan forming inside my head was wrong at every level, it was the only plan I had, and a plan meant some form of control.

My father's nickname for me was Sharkey because, much like a great white, it was impossible for me to stay still for any length of time. "Swim or die, Sharkey!" he'd yell as I was tearing through the kitchen. On my way to my next adventure, I was very aware that this meeting with Kimble may have been less of a plan, and more of a deliberate stall tactic on my part. A way to avoid mourning the loss of the case or thinking about what my next career move would be.

FOUR

Sweet Pea

"CAN I GET you another, Doll?" Sally Anne asked, pointing to my empty pint glass.

"No, thanks. I'm meeting someone soon and should probably be close to sober when she gets here."

"She? Some other woman trying to horn in on my man? Who's the bitch I have to cut?"

"You know my heart belongs to you alone. Besides, she's a lawyer, so you might want to rethink your knifing plan."

"Wouldn't be the first time I've been sued," she replied.

"She's with the DA's office."

"Wouldn't be my first time in jail either," she said, and I laughed. "Alright, honey. You just give me a holler if you need anything."

I gave Sally Anne a parting nod and checked my phone for any messages from Callie. Our meeting wasn't for another ten minutes, but I couldn't shake the feeling that she was gonna cancel at the last minute. However, I didn't have to worry for long. I looked up to see Callie, looking deadly as fuck, walking straight for the table.

She was dressed in a white sweater that clung tightly to her perfect body. A leather satchel was slung over her shoulder and the strap was positioned between her ample tits. She wore a black skirt and boots, showing off her long legs which I envisioned wrapped around me. She was a legitimate ten on any given day, but tonight her hotness level was off the fucking charts. God, I wanted to see her tied up.

I stood as she approached, but Callie spoke first.

"Thank you for meeting with me Mr. Kimb—"

"Sweet Pea," I interrupted. "My name is Sweet Pea. Charlie Kimble is dead, and I'd prefer he stay that way."

"Sorry," she said. "I'll be sure to remember that."

"Appreciate it."

"I take it you come here often," Callie said, scanning the room.

"Guilty as charged, counselor," I said, sounding corny as fuck. "Sorry, you probably hear shitty legal jokes all day long."

"Yup. Most of them from shitty lawyers," she said, breaking into a thousand-watt smile.

I laughed and tried not to stare. "Can I get you a drink?"

"Whiskey. Bourbon please. The older the better."

I let out a surprised chuckle. "Unexpected."

"What were you expecting?"

"Not sure, really. I guess vodka and passionfruit or something like that."

Callie raised an eyebrow. "Some sort of fruity 'chick' drink?"

"Well, yeah. I guess."

"Interesting."

"What's that?"

"You seemed like such a gentleman earlier, I hadn't pegged you as a sexist."

"I'm not sexist. It's just that most women I meet these days drink shit that looks like it belongs in a hummingbird feeder."

"Fair enough," Callie said with a smirk.

She'd just walked in and already she was busting my balls. Goddamn, she was hot.

I cleared my throat. "So, bourbon it is. Ice?"

"Neat please. Something old," she repeated.

"And by old, you mean expensive."

"Hey, you asked me to meet you here, remember?" Callie asked.

"After *you* asked *me* to coffee." I corrected.

"Which would have been much cheaper for you. You've now learned the first lesson about negotiating with me."

"What's that?" I asked.

"Always accept my first offer. It's the best one you're gonna get." Callie flashed another sly grin and my dick responded. Aggressively. This woman was going to be a fucking problem.

"Be right back," I said and headed for the bar. As much as I wanted to find out what the fuck Callie Ames wanted with me, I needed to step away and get my bearings. I was off balance and that was not normal for me.

Not on my bike, not in a fight, and not with women. Ever. I had to get my shit together, pronto.

"What's with the look? Your date stand you up?" Sally Anne asked as she wiped down the bar.

"What? No, she just got here. She's back at the table."

Sally Anne craned her neck in order to get a look at Callie.

"She's a pretty one," Sally Anne said. "Ya know, you could've called me over to your table to order. I wouldn't really have tried to scare her away."

"It's okay. To be honest with you, I'm not even sure what I'm doing here."

"In my experience, when one bellies up to the bar, it's usually to order a drink," Sally Anne teased.

"No, I mean why the fuck I'm here at all."

"Sorry, hun. I'm no good in the existential crisis department, but I can pour while you ponder."

"Uh, yeah. Bourbon. Something old."

"Don't think I've ever seen you drink bourbon before."

"It's for her," I motioned to the table. "She said not to come back with cheap shit because she'd know the difference."

"Pretty and she can drink? Maybe I won't stab her," she said, taking a bottle from the top shelf and pouring a stiff double.

"Jesus, Sally Anne. I said she wanted a drink, not cirrhosis."

"This is from my personal stock. If she's a real bourbon drinker, she'll love it."

"Thanks, babe. I'll take a young beer to go with that old bourbon as well."

I took a deep breath and "reset" before walking the drinks back to the table where I found Callie texting.

"Your boyfriend wondering where you are?" I asked.

"No, just a text from a work colleague."

"That little guy that was with you at the courthouse today?"

"His name is Rob, and he's not little," Callie replied.

"Defensive. So, he *is* your boyfriend."

"No. As a matter of fact, he is not. Not that we're here to discuss my personal life."

"Yeah, about that. Why are we here?" I asked, taking a sip of beer.

"I think I'll take a drink before answering that question," she said, bringing the glass to her nose. "A.H. Hirsch?"

"Holy shit," I said, nearly choking. "I guess you really do know your hooch."

"I can thank my father for my love of bourbon, baseball, and the law.

"Your dad a lawyer too?"

"A judge. He works in Marion County."

"You from there?"

"Born and raised in Aurora," Callie said, once again flashing that smile before taking a sip.

"A judge for a father? Shit, that must have been a laugh riot growing up," I said, trying to hide any trace of my desire to stand up, throw her over my shoulder, and take her to the upstairs crash pad. I imagined her tied up and waiting for me. I thought about which restraints I'd use and forced myself to stop there before I lost track of what Callie was saying.

"He was still a lawyer when I was little, but most of my life he's been the honorable Judge Ames."

"Is that why you went into law? To be like your old man?"

"Never consciously, but I suppose at some level I

wanted to be like him."

"You get along with your folks now?"

"Mom died when I was eleven. A car accident," she said softly.

"I'm sorry," I said. "That must have been pretty tough for you."

"Thank you. It was a long time ago," she replied, clearly trying to avoid the topic.

"I talk to my father a few times a week and as long as we stay away from the topic of politics, the Judge and I get along just fine."

"To healthy boundaries," I said raising my glass.

Callie giggled before taking another sip from her glass.

"What's so funny?" I asked.

"I guess I wasn't expecting a biker to raise a toast to the utilization of positive relationship tools."

"Is that your way of saying I'm not the knuckle dragger you thought I'd be?"

"I never thought that about you," Callie protested.

"Just that I was a psycho stalker."

"I never said 'psycho.'"

I chuckled. "Did you seriously think I was stalking you?"

"I first noticed you in the courthouse halls about eighteen months ago," Callie said.

"You *noticed* me? Who's been stalking who?"

"You're a little hard to miss," she countered.

I nodded. "Fair enough."

"Two weeks later, I saw you again, but this time it was in the courtroom of a case I was working."

"A custody case. The dad was a veteran with severe PTSD," I replied. "The mom was scared shitless. Fucking heartbreaking."

"That's right," Callie said softly. "And then again,

around six weeks after that."

"Brown vs. Hargrave."

Callie tilted her head. "You can see why I was concerned."

"Your hearings weren't the only ones I attended, you know?"

"I didn't know that at the time. All I knew was, every time I looked behind me, there was a giant biker lurking about."

"Lurking?" I laughed.

"Don't laugh at me," she said.

"I can't help it. You're funny."

"And you're a lurker." Callie swigged down the rest of her drink.

"Good stuff?" I asked.

"Just what the doctor ordered, thank you."

"Let's get you another round," I said.

"I just realized I've barely eaten anything today. I should probably get something in my stomach before I drink anymore."

"I know someone who can help out in that department," I said, flagging down Sally Anne.

FIVE

BURNING SAINTS

Callie

GIVEN MY CURRENT company and whereabouts, I probably should have been afraid. At the very least, I should have felt nervous, but I didn't. My line of work put me in the presence of true monsters on a regular basis, and my father had drilled into me at an early age to be cautious, wise, and discerning. My experience and instinct told me this man was not evil. I also knew he wasn't a saint, despite what his patch might say. Despite his gruff exterior, Sweet Pea had a softness in his eyes that no amount of scowling could hide. The patches on his vest told the story of a road warrior, but his eyes betrayed him, revealing glimpses of the deep waters that lay behind them.

"This place has the best potato salad you've ever had in your life," Sweet Pea said, motioning to a platinum blonde, middle-aged waitress, snapping me back to attention.

"What?" I asked.

"Potato salad. You need to eat. You said so yourself. You might not guess by lookin' at it, but the food here's really good." Sweet Pea handed me a menu as I continued to study him.

The waitress approached, and Sweet Pea introduced us.

"Ms. Callie Ames, this is Sally Anne. This is her place. Sally Anne, Ms. Callie Ames."

"Hey, how come you called her Ms., but I'm just plain ol' Sally Anne," she protested.

"My love, you are far from plain. Besides, you are the queen of this establishment and one should never refer to royalty as Ms.," Sweet Pea said, bowing his head.

Sally Anne rolled her eyes.

"I must beg your forgiveness for not addressing you as 'Her Royal Highness.'"

"Alright, knock it off, kiss ass. You two need some more drinks?"

"One more round for sure," Sweet Pea said, "But first, what's on the menu tonight?"

"If you're thinking about food, you should know Smokey's been working on ribs all day out back."

Before I could utter another word, Sweet Pea went into an ordering frenzy.

"Ribs, two racks," he said excitedly as he slapped his huge hand down on the table. "Two large potato salads, a half pan of cornbread…let's make that a full pan, Cajun tater tots, and—"

"Wait, I—"

"Oh, shit. You're not a vegan, are you?"

"No, but—"

"Good. And a big ol' plate of burnt ends."

"I'll freshen up your drinks too," Sally Anne said, and walked away before I could protest.

"We can't possibly eat all of that," I said.

"Oh, did you want me to order something for you too?" Sweet Pea smiled. It was within that smile that I realized for the first time that I wasn't just unafraid of Sweet Pea, I liked him. As in, I was attracted to him.

"Trust me. Smokey is a pit ninja," he said. "What this man does with meat is unbelievable."

I bet he's not the only one.

"It's just that I rarely eat like this, especially this late," I said, lying through my junk food chewing teeth.

"I can tell," he said, and gave me the once over.

Typically, if a man had ever brazenly eyed me up and down like that, I'd have tossed my drink in his face and walked out. Well, truthfully, I'd toss *his* drink in his face, finish mine, then walk out, but for whatever reason it didn't bother me when Sweet Pea looked at me. In fact, and it may have been the A.H. Hirsch kicking in, but I wanted him to do a lot more than look. Not that *that* could happen. *That* most certainly could not happen. *That* was off the table entirely.

"So, we've established I'm not a stalker, right?" Sweet Pea asked.

"After that dinner order, I'd say you pose a bigger threat to cows and pigs than to anyone at the courthouse."

Sweet Pea laughed. "What can I say? A growing boy needs to eat."

I'll give you something to eat, was all I could think of.

This man was seriously beginning to fry my brain. It had been a year since Carter and I had broken up, therefore a year since I'd last had sex. I wasn't one for casual hookups and typically reserved sex for men I was in a serious relationship with, but something about this guy made my pussy ache.

Instead of saying anything, I reached into my satchel, took out a file folder, and slid it across the table to Sweet Pea.

"What's this?"

"This is what I wanted to give you," I replied. I studied his face carefully as I watched him examine the folder's contents, my heart racing as I awaited his response. I wouldn't have to wait for long.

"What the fuck is this?" he growled, closing the file slowly.

"It's your life story, or at least what I know of it."

"I can see that, but why and how the fuck do you have this?"

"When I thought you might be stalking me, I had a P.I. find out everything they could about you."

"You hired a fucking private investigator to spy on me?" he snapped. "The girls at the Priest would love to meet you."

"I don't follow," I said, nervously.

"Some drag performers I know at the Pink Priest. I'm sure they'd love to get some tips. You could tell them exactly how you hide your massive balls in that tight skirt."

"Charming," I replied.

"Don't get pissy with me," he snapped. "This folder is full of pictures ranging from when I was a little kid to just a few months ago. Plus, my birth certificate, school records, all sorts of shit from my past. I need to know who this P.I. you hired is and where I can find him."

"I didn't hire anyone. I called in a favor with one of the agencies we work with on a regular basis to do a little digging on you. It's mostly harmless information anyway," I said.

"How the fuck do you know what's harmless in the hands of my enemies? There's information in here about my past, Callie. A past I left behind a long time ago and that I don't want anyone to know about."

"That's why I wanted to give it to you. Now that I know you're not a threat to me, there's no reason for me to keep any of this."

"And the P.I.?"

"I'm making it a point to stay out of your business, how about you stay out of mine?"

"Easy for you to say," he snapped. "You have a file on me."

"Not anymore," I countered.

"But you've read it."

"True."

"And?" Sweet Pea asked, his tone softening slightly.

"And what?"

"Find anything interesting?"

"As a matter of fact, I did," I said, shifting in my seat uncomfortably, but saying nothing more.

"Jesus, Callie. You gonna tell me what this is all about or not?"

My heart raced and beads of sweat formed on my brow as my internal struggle raged on. I really wished I had more bourbon but forced myself to reveal the horrible truth of why we were here, anyway. "I want John Knight to pay for what he did."

"Of course, you do," Sweet Pea replied. "I'm sure you put everything you had into that case. But what does that have to do with me?"

"I failed Elsie Miller once and I'm not going to fail

her again," I said, the fear in my voice giving way to anger.

"What are you saying, Callie?"

"I'm saying I know all about you and your club, and I want to hire you for your services."

"Are you serious?" Sweet Pea asked. "Do you think I'm a fucking moron? This has got to be the worst set up in the history of the D.A.'s office."

"This isn't about my job. The legal system has already failed Elsie. I'm coming to you for justice. This file is an offering of good faith."

"Why the hell would a lawyer come to a biker, one she recently suspected of being her stalker, to deal with a pedophile?"

"It's not like I had planned any of this. I thought tonight I'd be having celebratory drinks with Rob. But after the verdict was read and Knight walked free, something inside of me broke. And then he was on the courthouse steps going on about forgiving the family for their sins. As soon as I saw you on the steps, I knew what I had to do if I was ever going to get justice for Elsie."

"What is it exactly you think I do for a living, counselor?"

"What am I supposed to say? Am I supposed to act all innocent? Like I don't know anything about your *lifestyle*?"

"What you call my lifestyle, I call my life, and I don't think you know the first goddamned thing about it, regardless of what it says in this file," he replied, tossing the folder across the table to me.

"I didn't mean to offend you," I said.

"You haven't offended me. You've pissed me off," he said, without a trace of anger in his voice. From what I could tell, Sweet Pea wasn't a man who was easily rattled. "Besides, there's a lot more to me and my club than what's in that little file of yours."

"For instance?" I asked.

"You think I'm gonna tell you anything about club business?" He laughed.

"You brought it up," I challenged.

"No. What I said was, if you knew anything about my club, you'd know exactly how shitty your plan is."

I studied Sweet Pea's face carefully, looking for traces of deception, but found none. Determining whether someone is lying to you is possibly the greatest asset a trial attorney can have. My father was a human polygraph. I was better than most, but not without my blind spots. There were many things about Sweet Pea that caused me to believe him, but I was also acutely aware that I *wanted* to believe him, and that made me nervous as hell.

"I'd ask if I can get you anything else, but I don't think there's anything left in the kitchen," Sally Anne said as she arrived with our food. Our order was so large, Sally Anne had to be accompanied by another waitress with a full tray of her own. Our drinks were once again refreshed and the giant spread, laid out before us.

"Thanks, Doll. Everything looks amazing," Sweet Pea said, flashing his dimples at Sally Anne before she left us alone again.

"How are we possibly going to eat all of this?" I asked, hoping to reset the conversation.

"I should probably take mine to go," Sweet Pea said, taking out his wallet.

"What? Hold on," I protested, as he stood.

"I appreciate your company and the file, but you can keep it, along with your job offer. I'm not for hire and I'm not for sale." He pulled out five one hundred-dollar bills and placed them on the table. "I hope you enjoy the rest of your meal and your evening."

* * *

Sweet Pea

I left Callie Ames and her file at the Burning Saints' private table and headed for the rear exit.

"Wait a minute," she protested, but I kept on walking, paying her no mind. Well, pretending to pay her no mind. Presently, I couldn't imagine how the fuck I was going to get her out of my head.

I'd almost made it to the door at the end of the narrow hallway, when someone shoved me from behind. I spun around, ready to clock the fool who'd put his hands on me and was shocked to see Callie standing there.

"What the fuck?" I asked, surprised not only by her actions, but by how hard she shoved me.

"What the fuck, *me*? What the fuck, *you!*" she replied, her arms stretched out in a 'come at me bro' stance.

I burst out in laughter, which was apparently not the reaction Callie was looking for.

"We're not done talking," she said, scowling.

"I see how it is," I said, folding my arms.

"How *what* is?"

"You're a fightin' drunk," I replied.

"First of all, I'm not a drunk," Callie argued. "And what does my drinking have to do with you being rude and walking away like that?"

"I'm not being rude, I'm trying to save you," I replied.

"Save me. From what?"

"From saying or doing anything more stupid than you've already done tonight."

42

Callie began to speak, as if ready to fire off her next arguing remark, but instead paused before saying, "You're wrong."

"About what?"

"I can get a lot more stupid. Drinking doesn't put me in the mood for fighting," she said, closing the distance between us.

"No?" I asked, looking down into her eyes.

"It puts me in the mood to fuck."

Jesus, fuck!

I smiled slowly. "Your place or mine?"

SIX

BURNING SAINTS

Callie

WE'D BEEN INSIDE my apartment for approximately three seconds before the first article of clothing hit the floor and within moments, Sweet Pea and I had managed to strip each other completely bare. He was an amazing kisser and my pussy ached as we stood together, exploring each other's mouths.

Normally, I'd be way more "up in my head" about being with a man for the first time, but I simply had no time to be self-conscious. I wanted Sweet Pea to fuck me, right here, right now. No, I *needed* Sweet Pea to fuck me.

"Jesus, you're gorgeous," he hissed, his mouth moving along my collarbone.

I wove my fingers into his hair just as he wrapped an arm around my waist and jumped about a foot with a growl.

"Holy shit!" Sweet Pea suddenly yelled, pointing to our feet. "What the fuck is that?"

I looked down to see Ruby making her way through the living room.

"Don't be afraid, it's just Ruby," I said.

"That's a fucking snake. A giant fucking snake," Sweet Pea exclaimed.

"Don't tell me a big tough biker like yourself is afraid of a little ol' reptile," I said, bending to pick her up.

"Little? That thing is a fucking monster!"

"You're going to hurt her feelings," I admonished, stroking her scaly skin. "She's a total sweetheart, even though she's not supposed to be out of her house." I carried Ruby back to her aquarium and settled her back inside.

"Why the fuck do you have that thing?"

"Ruby's not a thing, she's a ball python and she's a great pet. She's low maintenance, doesn't need a ton of attention, and she's an excellent listener."

Sweet Pea looked unconvinced. "I can't get over a woman like you keeping something like a snake around for conversation."

"Women have been talking with snakes since the Garden of Eden, ya know?" I pointed out.

"Yeah and look where that shit got us."

I laughed and made my way back to Sweet Pea.

"I'm not fuckin' you in front of your snake, Callie," he said.

"Chicken," I retorted,

"I won't fuck you in front of a chicken either."

I laughed, taking his hand and leading him up to my bedroom. Pushing open the door, I led him inside and chuckled when he closed the door, pushing it hard, making sure it latched closed.

His lips claimed mine again in another hot, hungry kiss. I ran my hands up his muscled abs as his lips kissed their way to my ear. "How much prep do you need, counselor?" he asked, then his tongue ran along the seam of my lips.

"How much do you want?"

"I need to be inside you."

"I need that too," I breathed out, and he kissed me. I bit his lower lip and he spun me to face the wall, pulling my hips toward him. I anchored my hands to the plaster in order not to fall over and heard the tearing of foil as he messed with a condom, but then I felt his cock at my entrance, and he pushed in slowly. Lordy, he was big.

No surprise there, but he was bigger than I'd ever had, so my body needed a minute to adjust. Lucky for me, he seemed to understand and slowed his movements.

"Spread, Callie," he instructed, and I spread, which took him deeper, and he groaned as his dick slid to the hilt.

He buried himself deep again and then moved in and out, picking up speed and I whimpered with each thrust as I felt an orgasm threatening to spill. Oh my god, I'd never felt like this before. Sex had never been this good.

"Sweet Pea," I screamed, unable to stop my climax, my pussy clamping his dick, hard.

He squeezed my hips, his fingers digging deliciously into my flesh as he slammed into me harder and harder and then I felt him swell before his dick pulsed and emptied into me.

He gave my ass a gentle smack and slid out of me. "I'll be right back, but we're not done."

I nodded, trying to catch my breath as he left me leaning against the wall. Oh my word, what the hell had I just done?

And how soon could we do it again?

* * *

Sweet Pea

I stepped into the bathroom, got rid of the condom, then headed back into the bedroom to find Callie stretching out on her bed.

"Where did your name come from?" Callie asked as I lay down next to her.

"Sweet Pea?"

She nodded.

"Cutter started calling me that from just about day one."

"Your old President?"

I smiled and nodded. "When I first came out here, Ropes was more like a dad to me than a brother. I guess in some ways he always was. It took us a while to figure out how to just be brothers. We're probably still figuring some of that shit out. Anyway, Cutter kept saying me and Ropes reminded him of Pop-Eye and Sweet Pea. You know, a tough dude with muscles, taking care of a scrawny little blonde kid."

"I can't imagine you were ever scrawny," Callie said, her hand going to my chest.

"Yeah, well I was, and from then on the name just stuck. By the time I was patched in, nobody even bothered bringing up a new name for me."

"I think it's the perfect name for you," she said, giving me a kiss.

47

"I'm glad you like it," I replied.

"And I'm glad you're not scrawny anymore," she said, her hand moving to my cock.

"Not so fast," I warned, and knelt between her legs, grinning as I ran a finger through her slick wetness, spreading it on her clit and rolling the hard nub under my fingertip. She moaned, her back arched and I leaned down to blow gently as I slid two fingers inside of her.

"You like this, counselor?"

I barely recognized my voice. I'm typically demonstrative, commanding, but with her, my tone was gentle, raspy, and my dick was instantly hard again with her spread out before me, her bare tits so close to my mouth. Jesus.

"Yes," Callie whispered. "Keep going."

"Oh, I plan to," I promised.

I had no intention of stopping as I spread her legs wide and buried my face between her lush folds. I lapped at her pussy, devouring her, memorizing her smell, her taste, and her softness. I slid my fingers back inside of her and felt her walls begin to pulse around them, so I pulled away and rolled on a condom, hovering over her and kissing her as I buried myself deep.

She let out a quiet mew and wrapped her legs around me, digging her nails into my ass in a silent invitation to fuck her.

So, fuck her I did, and the harder I slammed into her the more she wanted.

"Baby, I don't want to hurt you," I panted out as I buried my dick to the hilt.

She squeezed my ass, pulling me closer to her. "You're not. Harder, Sweet Pea. Please. I'll tell you if it's too much."

I kissed her, rolling a nipple between my finger and thumb before giving it a tight pinch, as I slammed into her, and she screamed my name as her body shuddered and her pussy squeezed my dick so hard, I couldn't help but come. I couldn't believe this woman had fuckin' milked me twice in less than twenty minutes, and it had been straight sex.

* * *

Callie

So, *that* just happened.

"Your place is nice," Sweet Pea said, his words tethering me back to reality.

"Hmmm?"

"Your apartment," he replied. "We got right down to business as soon as we came in. Then there was the whole 'me almost getting eaten by your roommate' thing. I never got the chance to compliment you on your place."

I rolled over on Sweet Pea's chest to face him. "You're a strange little biker, aren't you?"

Sweet Pea laughed so hard, I thought he might break a rib. "Hell, woman. I've been called a lot of things, but to my knowledge, never that."

"Well, what kind of hard-core biker compliments a woman on her interior decorating after hooking up?"

"First of all, I was speaking more from an architectural standpoint. Secondly, was I just some cheap hookup to you?" Sweet Pea asked, looking hurt.

"Oh. My god, no. That's not what I meant. That was amazing…you were amazing."

Sweet Pea smiled wide.

"You're teasing me," I said, feeling my face flush. "See, that's the kind of strange behavior I'm talking about."

"What?"

"Whenever I ask you a question about yourself, you either respond monosyllabically, poetically, or with a joke."

Sweet Pea remained smiling, but I could feel him stiffen and he said nothing in response.

"Or, you say nothing at all," I said.

Sweet Pea sat up and we were now facing each other on my bed. The glow from the light in the master bath illuminating our naked bodies. I reached for a sheet to cover myself, but Sweet Pea's hand stopped me. "Stay just like that. I want to see all of you."

"Don't look too close, you'll find all of my flaws," I said with a laugh. Sweet Pea didn't laugh back.

"Please don't do that," he said tenderly.

"Sorry. It's hard not to feel a little…well, naked like this." I said.

"Good, then you know how I fuckin' feel."

"What do you mean?"

"Callie, you said I avoid questions about myself, but you already have a file on me. You had an investigator spy on me and dig into my past. Do you know how fucked up that is?"

"Yes, and I feel bad."

"You've had the upper hand since we met, and that's not something I'm used to or comfortable with. I shouldn't have to be the only one who's an open book here."

"Does getting me into bed balance the scales?" I asked, once again reaching for the sheets.

"Don't do that," he said, "And don't put words in my mouth."

Once again, as much as I fought the urge, I could only think about everything of mine I'd enjoy putting in his mouth.

"All I'm saying is, you know a hell of a lot about

me, and I know next to nothing about you."

"I don't think that's fair," I said. "I think I made myself pretty vulnerable when I offered you money to...*you know.*"

"Kill John Knight," Sweet Pea said plainly.

"Shhhhhh. I never said I wanted you to *kill him,*" I whispered.

"We'll get back to that. I'm not done talking about the file."

"I told you why I had it and that I was sorry. Plus, I gave it back to you," I reminded him.

"But you read it, and something in that file convinced you that I could be hired to do your dirty work."

"It's not like I read your diary or something. Most of the file is made up of records of Charles Kimble, which abruptly cut off at age fourteen."

"I'm quite aware of when Charles Kimble died," he said.

"But he didn't die. He just vanished one day. The Kimble family gave vague excuses regarding his absence from the public eye, until one day, the public simply stopped asking altogether. And now I find out you're here, in Portland."

"You make me sound like the goddamned Lindbergh baby. Plenty of kids leave home and don't go back."

"So, you're saying it's normal for both sons of a prominent business tycoon to leave home as teenagers and join a biker gang?"

"I don't know about *normal,* but it's what happened."

"What about everything and everyone you left behind?"

"The only person that I left behind that matters is Charles Kimble."

"Please let me assure you. There's nothing normal

about wiping your identity and walking away from a family fortune."

"So, you figured I must be some sort of ghost assassin for hire? Is that what your private dick told you? If so, you need to ask him for your money back."

"What my investigator came back with has nothing to do with why I asked you for help with Knight," I replied.

"Then why did you come to me?"

"Because you ride with the Burning Saints."

"So, I'm in a club? Big deal."

"You forget that I work in the D.A.'s office, which means I'm more than familiar with every criminal organization in the Portland metro area. I know exactly who the Burning Saints are and more importantly how they make their money."

"How's that?"

"Protection," I replied.

Sweet Pea's dimples were on full display as he grinned. "You've got this all figured out, don't you counselor?"

"No, but someone has to do something."

"So, what? You're a blood thirsty vigilante now?"

"You make me sound like I'm hatching an evil plot," I said standing.

"Well, aren't you?"

"I'm not the monster. You know all too well exactly what Knight did to Elsie."

"What the fuck is that supposed to mean?" Sweet Pea's tone turned more serious and his posture stiffened.

"You were in court. You heard her testimony for yourself," I replied.

"Of course, I know Knight is a monster, but you're not. You're a lawyer. Not a judge or a one-woman jury, and you're sure as hell not an executioner. Especially if you're not even willing to do the job yourself."

"I told you I never said I wanted him dead," I repeated.

"Then what? You want I should break his legs boss?" He said in a 1940s mobster voice.

"Can you please not joke around about this?"

"I'm as serious as a crowbar to the skull, Callie," Sweet Pea said rising to his feet. His naked body on glorious display. "Is that what you want me to do to Knight? Take a crowbar and bash his fucking brains in? Or how about I break his kneecaps? It's your dime after all. What do you want, Callie?"

"I want Knight to pay for what he did. I want justice!" I shouted.

"There's no justice if you have blood on your hands," Sweet Pea said, walking to me and pulling me to his chest. He held me as the dam of my emotions broke wide open and I began to sob uncontrollably. It was only at this moment in Sweet Pea's arms that I'd realized where my anger had driven me. This morning, I was a sworn champion of the law, by mid-day I'd hatched a crazy scheme to have Knight roughed up by a biker, and by the nighttime I was having mind-blowing sex with that same biker. I'd heard of grief making people do crazy things, but I must truly be out of my mind.

"Oh, my God," I said, wiping my face with my arm. "What am I doing?" I asked pathetically.

"Looks to me like you're losing your shit, counselor," Sweet Pea said, his trademark smile returning.

"I'd love to argue your point, but I'm compelled to agree with your assessment of the situation."

Sweet Pea lifted my chin, his piercing blue eyes meeting mine. "Feel whatever you need to feel, Callie. You're allowed. A guy I respect a lot once told me, 'Your feelings belong to you, but your actions belong to the world.'"

"Who was that?" I asked, once again surprised by the words of Sweet Pea, the philosopher poet.

"Someone I think you should meet. A friend of mine named Cowboy. I think he might be able to help you with some of the emotions you're feeling."

"How's that?"

"Cowboy is the president of a club called Bikers for Kids. They're a charity organization that does a lot of work with kids like Elsie Miller and her family. Children that are abused who need someone to stand up for them. They try to be a voice for the voiceless. I think you'd like them. Cowboy was angry, too, so he decided to do something about it."

"And you think the two of us should meet?"

"I do. As a matter of fact, a couple of the Saints have been out on a charity run with BFK and should be getting back to town any time. They're staying at the Sanctuary. Maybe you could stop by tomorrow after church and I could introduce you before they head out of town."

"Sure," I said with a yawn, starting to feel the effects of a full-blown adrenaline dump. "But I'm still not sure why."

"I meant what I said back at Sally Anne's. There's a lot about my club you don't know."

"I'm not dumb, Sweet Pea. A lot of motorcycle clubs do charitable work in order to look good in their communities."

"What I'm talking about goes deeper than that," he said softly. "How about you climb back into bed. I want to show you something."

I did as Sweet Pea instructed as he went out to the living room, returning with his black leather motorcycle vest.

"This is my kutte. It's the most important thing in the world to me," he said.

"It's very sexy," I said.

"This isn't a fashion accessory. It's a statement of who I am and who I belong to. It's my suit of armor and my coat of arms."

"I think I understand, but why are you showing it to me?"

"I have two new patches on my kutte. Do you know which ones they are?" he asked, holding the kutte up next to him.

"It's a little hard to tell given the lack of light, but the Road Captain one looks a little brighter than the others."

"A new promotion," he replied.

"Congratulations," I said.

"The other is this one," he said pointing to a circular patch containing a backwards R and an H.

"What's that one signify?"

"Not a big fan of hard rock music?"

"Big band mostly," I replied, to which Sweet Pea chuckled.

"Jesus, Callie. Do you have any tastes that don't match those of an eighty-year old man?"

"Not really," I admitted.

"This is the logo for the band RatHound, but that's not really what's important. What is important is the patch that it's covering up."

"What's that?"

"A one-percenter patch," he said. "Do you know what that is?"

I nodded.

"So, you know what it means?"

I nodded again. "Why is it covered up?"

"I can't go into any details about club business, but

I'll tell you this, the Burning Saints are no longer a one-percenter club. When Cutter died, the past died with him."

"I think our justice system would disagree with you," I said, another yawn escaping.

"Perhaps, but the point is our club is no longer a "criminal organization" as you put it. The Saints have started and invested in businesses all around town and are no longer running the protection game in Portland."

"Who is?"

"I told you, I can't discuss club matters, but I will see you tomorrow. How does eleven o'clock sound?"

"As long as I can sleep in until 8:00, I'm golden," I slurred.

"Good. I'll see you after church, then. I'm gonna take off and let you sleep," he said, tucking me in with a gentle kiss on the forehead.

I was utterly drained from the events of the past twenty-four hours. I was sure that I'd never experienced such a roller coaster of a day and prayed I'd not see another like if for a long time.

SEVEN

Sweet Pea

I AWOKE DISORIENTED to the sound of bikes passing through the Sanctuary gates. I couldn't tell exactly how many, but from the sheer volume of the pipes, I'd guess around a dozen. Unaware if the riders were friend or foe, I pulled the pistol I had hidden underneath my mattress and quietly got out of bed.

After Wolf's "resignation" from the Saints, and Kitty's subsequent reaction, Minus had instructed Clutch to collect and lock up any and all guns. Only those on guard duty would be armed. No exceptions. Minus feared the Spiders would be looking for any opportunity to ignite the war between us, and guns only increased the chances of violence happening in the streets of Portland. He was probably right but there was no way in hell I was gonna ride unarmed. Especially now. I figured whatever Minus would do to me if he found my gun couldn't be worse than finding myself in a gunfight without a gun.

I glanced at the clock on my nightstand and was surprised to see it was 10:00 am. I never slept in this late, but a severe case of cottonmouth and a raging headache reminded me of how much I drank last night, not to mention everything else that went down. Jesus, what the fuck was I thinking?

I walked to the opposite side of the room to look out the window, but three loud raps on my door caused me to spin around and take aim.

Two more thumps.

I pulled back the hammer and held my breath.

"Pea, you in there?" my brother, Ropes called out, causing me to exhale and lower my weapon. "The guys are back from the run. Church is starting soon."

"Yeah, be right there," I replied, relieved I wasn't going to have to engage in gunplay while battling a hangover.

I put the gun back in its hiding place, got dressed, and joined Ropes and the others outside. A small group of Saints had just returned from a charity run with the Bikers for Kids, including Doozer, one of the three soldiers under my newly appointed command along with Spike and Tacky.

Doozer was the club's youngest but most promising member, and I saw him as the little brother I never had. He was patched in on his twenty-third birthday after only eight months of being a prospect. He was loyal to the club, more than capable with his hands, and was as charming as the Devil himself. The club had high hopes for him, and I was more than happy to have him as one of my soldiers.

Presently, Doozer appeared to be laying his famous charm on one of the BFK's more intriguing members, a pretty young rider named Trouble. They were currently standing hip to hip, leaning against Doozer's bike, arms around each other, seemingly unaware of the swirling chaos of bikes and bikers surrounding them. It was painfully obvious that Doozer had only volunteered to go on the run to spend time with Trouble, not that she seemed to mind.

"They been like this during the whole trip?" I asked, approaching Cowboy, the BFK's President.

"Only the entire fucking time," he responded dryly.

"They seem…happy."

"I know. It's fucking weird. I didn't even know Trouble knew how to smile."

I laughed. "He keep his hands off her ass long enough to be of any use to you out there?"

"He's a good soldier. He stayed sharp on the road, did as he was told, and the kids loved him wherever we went."

"Oh, yeah?"

"Every foster home and hospital we went to, he was the first one in the door. He wore that fuckin' elf suit every time and never complained once."

"I'm sure he'll be happy to add 'Santa's Helper' to his resume." I chuckled.

"Minus says everything's been quiet here," Cowboy said, changing the subject from budding love to potential war.

"So far," I replied. "Maybe even a little too quiet."

"How so?"

"Wolf and I have history. I know him probably better than anyone, and he's never this quiet for this long."

"His silence making you nervous?"

"Itchy as fuck. Wolf is impulsive and loud. He's never restrained and rarely unpredictable, so the fact that he and the Spiders have gone underground since our standoff can only mean bad news."

"We have your backs if shit jumps off," Cowboy said.

"The Saints know and appreciate that, brother."

I shook Cowboy's hand and made my way to Doozer and Trouble, clearing my throat as I neared the happy couple."

"Hey, Sweet Pea," Doozer said, straightening up his posture as I approached. "You remember Trouble, don't you?"

"Of course," I replied, turning to her. "This guy isn't giving you a hard time, is he?"

"I'd kick his ass if he tried," she replied, and although she was smirking while she said it, I believed her.

Bikers for Kids was a unique club, in that its members shared a singular goal of caring for children suffering from abuse. Their club did everything from fund raising to physically protecting families from their abusers. BFK was not afraid to confront their enemies, and the Gresham Spiders, a club notorious for trafficking, prostitution, and dealing drugs in schools, were certainly on its list.

Not surprising, many of the BFK's members had suffered their own forms of trauma and abuse as children. It was something I had in common with them, but not a fact that I chose to disclose. Besides, I'd dealt with my past and was more than happy to leave it where it was, far the fuck behind me.

"Cowboy said the run went well."

"Those kids, man." Doozer said with a sad smile. "Some of their stories really tore me up, ya know? I can't believe how brave those kids are after all the shit they've gone through."

"I'm glad you went," I said and patted Doozer on the back. I meant what I said too.

Doozer was almost as tall as me. Way leaner, but just as tough. Yet, despite his rough exterior, he had a good heart. It's what I valued the most in him. He reminded me of a younger, less jaded version of myself. Not that I was a grumpy old man or anything. Hell, I was only four or five years older than my soldiers but had already ridden or been dragged down some rough roads.

"Where are Spike and Tacky?" Doozer asked, looking around.

"Out on patrol, but they should be back any time now," I replied.

"Hey, I wanna talk to you about something if you've got a second," Doozer said.

"Church in five!" Minus called out.

"I'm all yours, but can we talk after church?" I asked. "I need to get something in my tank before the meeting starts."

"No problem," he said.

I left the two lovebirds alone and headed to the kitchen where I found Ropes and Clutch engaged in a lively conversation at the coffee maker.

"What the fuck was I supposed to say?" Ropes asked.

"I don't know, but something better than 'oops.' I mean, you're the fucking writer," Clutch replied.

"Exactly! I'm a writer. I need *some* time to formulate my words. I had zero time to process what the hell was happening. I walked into the room and there she was on the bed, naked, covered in oil."

"On all fours, with a rainbow, ponytail dildo in her

ass?"

"A butt plug actually, but we didn't know that at the time."

"We?" Clutch asked excitedly.

"Oh yeah. Devlin was standing right there next to me the entire time."

"What the fuck kind of conversation did I just walk in on?" I asked, stopping dead in my tracks.

"Your brother was just telling me about a reader that managed to sneak into his hotel room at the last signing event he attended," Clutch said. "Apparently, she wanted to play pony with Mr. Morningwood here. Unfortunately, the wife was with him."

"Wrong," Ropes said. "This little filly wanted to play with both Mr. *and* Mrs. Morningwood."

"Oh, shit!" Clutch shouted. "So was the answer yea or *neigh*?"

"I think you can imagine what Devlin's response was to this young woman's presence."

Clutch silently sipped his coffee.

"I will say, it was highly entertaining watching Devlin attempt to wrestle this completely lubed up chick out the door," Ropes laughed. "That's actually when we found out her tail was attached to a toy. Devlin had almost shoved her through the doorway when it sort of... popped out."

"Don't you mean pooped out?" Clutch asked, much to his own amusement.

"This sort of shit happen to you all the time?" I asked.

"I've seen things at signings that make our club parties look like Boy Scout meetings," he replied.

I poured myself a large glass of what my club brothers referred to as "sludge" and made my way to the Sanctuary's chapel. Sludge was a homemade juice made from fruits and vegetables, mixed with protein powder and fish oils. It looked, smelled, and tasted horrendous, but gave me all the nutrients I needed, and best of all, remained untouched in the refrigerator by my brothers.

"Thanks again to everyone for your help with this year's toy drive," Minus said, motioning to our guests from the Bikers for Kids. "Cowboy had great things to say about the trip. I'm grateful for the friendship between our two clubs, and to have helped out just a little this holiday season."

"The Saints are welcome to ride with us anytime," Cowboy replied.

"Alright then," Minus said, turning his attention back to us. "Now that Christmas is over and the fat man has flown back to the elf sweatshop, let's get down to business."

Minus spent the next few minutes going over a few pieces of general club business before turning to the topic on everyone's mind.

"We still haven't heard a word from the Spiders. If they've backed down, they haven't made it known, but they also haven't retaliated either."

"You think Wolf is still gonna make a play against us after the other night?" I asked.

"I'm staying hopeful," Minus replied.

"You don't sound convinced," Ropes said.

"You know Wolf," he countered. "He ever come across as the backin' down type to you?"

"No, but do you really think he wants to go to war? Especially with all the other area clubs standing with us?" My brother countered.

"I think if he had it his way, Wolf would have sounded the battle cry the night we showed up at their clubhouse, but Char is still calling the shots, and even Wolf isn't dumb enough to disobey him."

"You think Char is more afraid of us than Wolf is?"

"I don't think Char is afraid of anything. I just know he's smarter than Wolf."

"How's that?" I asked.

"When Char went to prison, he had to choose an acting president to run things on the outside. He needed someone that was ambitious and ruthless but could be controlled, and Wolf fit the bill perfectly in every way but one."

"He wasn't a Spider," I said.

"I'm betting Char was smart enough to recognize that no one within the Spiders' ranks would best serve his purpose, so even though Wolf was a Saint, he lured him away with bait he knew Wolf couldn't resist."

"What?"

"Power," he replied.

"Wolf definitely wants to be The Man, but how is making him acting president smart on Char's part? I mean, why have a power-hungry employee mind your store while you're gone?"

"Because power is blinding, and Char has been around long enough to know that. He can use the club's presidency as the ultimate carrot to motivate Wolf."

"What if Char's wrong and Wolf tries to overthrow him?"

"Then I'm sure he'll have no problem switching from carrot to stick. Char's dug more graves in the Eastern Oregon desert than he can remember. Either way, this is Wolf's first test as acting president and how he handles it will be crucial to his survival within the Spiders' ranks."

"Char is dead," Clutch said.

"Tough talk isn't worth shit right now, Clutch," Minus snapped.

"No, I mean Char is *dead*," he said pointing to his

phone. "Eldie just texted me a news article." Clutch slid his phone across the table to Minus.

"Holy shit," he said, reading a portion of the article out loud. "The president and founder of the notorious biker gang, the Gresham Spiders, Harrold "Char" Carsen, was found stabbed to death in his Multnomah County prison cell late last night. His cellmate, George Yonko, is being held in solitary confinement as the chief suspect of the gruesome murder. The motive for Mr. Carsen's killing is currently unknown to authorities."

"Holy shit," I replied.

Minus sat silently stroking his beard.

"What are you thinking, Prez?" Clutch asked.

"I'm thinking Wolf and Char had a disagreement on how to handle our dispute, and Wolf found a way to deal with it."

"You really think Wolf would do that? Kill his own club's founder? That would be suicide," Clutch argued.

"Only if he didn't get support from within the Spiders' ranks. But what if he did? For all we know, their club is filled with guys that would love to put a knife in Char's back themselves. He wasn't a good guy, not even to his own people, so who the fuck knows? If Wolf is behind the assassination, we can only assume Char wanted to make peace and Wolf has other ideas."

"He probably paid off or threatened Char's cellmate to do the job," Ropes said.

Clutch chimed in. "Fuck Char. He was a smut peddling piece of shit and the world's better off without him."

"That's true, but he was the only one holding Wolf's chain. Without Char's leadership and restraint, the Spiders are now at the complete control of a pissed off, blood thirsty lunatic."

Just then, Doozer came through the door. "Sorry, I

didn't want to interrupt."

"What's up, Doozer," Minus asked.

"There's someone at the gate for Sweet Pea," he said, then addressed me personally. "She said she's your lawyer."

Clutch shot me a look, that if weaponized, could easily take care of our Wolf problem.

"We keeping you from something important, Sweet Pea?" Minus asked.

"Shit. I'm sorry," I said. "I'll be right back." I slinked out the door, right behind Doozer, into the hallway.

"What the fuck? Never interrupt church unless it's life or death," I said, backhanding his chest.

"I know, but I figured it was important. She said she was your lawyer and that you told her to meet you here. Here, she gave me this," Doozer said, holding out one of Callie's business cards. "Sorry, Pea. I didn't mean to jam you up with Minus."

"No, it's okay. Where is she?"

"She's still outside the gate. No one gets in without officer approval right now, that's why I came and got you."

I arrived to find Callie outside the gate with Socks, who was currently on guard duty. Callie was holding a large pink baker's box. It was opened wide and Socks was currently peering inside.

"Sorry I'm a little early. I brought pastries," Callie said with a smile as I approached.

"Get your ass back in that guard tower," I bellowed at Socks, who quickly grabbed something covered in chocolate from the box before returning to his post.

EIGHT

BURNING SAINTS

Callie

SWEET PEA DIDN'T look happy.

"Hey, Callie, this isn't really a good time. We're in the middle of something—"

"You did say to come by today, right?" I asked.

"Yeah, but I—"

"Good. I was a little nervous that maybe you didn't really mean everything you said last night."

By 'nervous,' what I really meant was I'd had four complete nervous breakdowns since my eyes sprang open at five o'clock this morning. I tried, unsuccessfully to go back to sleep, but everything I'd said and done kept replaying over and over in my mind. Whatever was left of my mind, anyway. By six forty-five, I gave up, got dressed, and hit my favorite bakery for some sanity pastries. While I was at the bakery, I got the bright idea to grab a couple dozen goodies to bring with me. Sweet Pea did say the Burning Saints had church this morning, and although I was fairly sure their version of church differed greatly from mine, who didn't like pastries? Now I was holding a bright pink box while standing at the gate of a biker gang compound like a total goober.

I couldn't believe I'd slept with Sweet Pea, but even more shocking was how bad I wanted to do it again now that he was standing in front of me. I was self-aware enough to know this fling with the big, bad, biker was probably nothing more than a distraction from dealing with the dumpster fire that was my career, but a big part of me simply didn't care. I told Sweet Pea I would be here and so I'd arrived, on time, pastries in hand.

"No, Callie, that's not it. Last night was great."

"Good, then let me in. My arms are getting tired."

"It's really not a good time," he said, glancing behind him.

"So, you're definitely blowing me off."

"When I invited you to stop by, I thought we'd be done with church by now. I'm not sure I was thinking too clearly last night, to tell you the truth."

"The truth would be nice," I replied.

"Look, I'm being straight with you, it's just that…" Sweet Pea stopped, momentarily distracted by Socks in the guard tower, who was looking intently down at us. He stared at us silently, chewing his pastry as if he were watching his favorite soap opera.

"Mind your own fuckin' business," Sweet Pea snapped up at him before turning back to me. "This isn't your fault."

"I never said it was my fault and fortunately this

whole mix-up can easily be rectified by you opening this gate and letting me in," I said.

Before Sweet Pea could respond, a voice called out from behind him.

"You hired an attorney, huh? You gonna sue the doctor that botched your penis enlargement surgery?"

"Shit," Sweet Pea muttered before spinning around to the approaching biker.

"Everything's cool. We were just saying goodbye," Sweet Pea said.

"Were we?" I asked.

"Seems like there's a little confusion with Mrs..."

"Clutch, this is Callie Ames, the attorney I told you about. Callie, this is Clutch, the Burning Saints' Sergeant at Arms."

"Pleased to meet you," Clutch said curtly. "We're just thrilled that Sweet Pea spends so much of his free time hanging out with Lady Justice."

Sweet Pea remained silent, but the looks he was exchanging with his superior officer said it all.

"What brings you to the Sanctuary this morning, Mrs. Ames?" Clutch asked, his charm barely masking the irritation in his voice.

"It's *Ms.* Ames, and I'm here because Sweet Pea invited me. An invitation I'd happily accept if he'd let me in."

"Did he? Sweet Pea invited you?" Clutch asked in an exaggerated tone. "Dear brother, why are you being so rude to an invited guest by making her wait outside? Look, she comes bearing gifts."

Sweet Pea glared at Clutch for a few moments before motioning up to Socks. The electronically controlled gate rolled open just wide enough for me and the pastries to gain passage and I slipped through.

"There, that's better," Clutch said with a huge smile

as the gate closed behind me.

"Thank you for your help. I've got this handled," Sweet Pea said to Clutch through his tight sneer. "Why don't you take these refreshments back to church and I'll join you in a minute?" he said practically shoving the box into Clutch's chest.

"Be sure you do, brother," Clutch said before turning on his heels and walking away.

"Well, that sure was pleasant," I said, addressing the obvious tension between the two men.

"Yeah, he's a little pissed off at me right now."

"Couldn't tell," I said dryly.

"Clutch is a good guy, he's just got a lot going on," he said, in a tone of 'brotherly defensiveness.'

"Hopefully, the goodies help," I said, trying to lighten the mood a little.

"Look, Callie. Shit's pretty tense around here right now and inviting a total stranger to come around probably wasn't my smartest move."

"No offense taken," I said.

"I meant you're a stranger to the club, not to me," he said, taking my hand, his voice softening. "I meant it when I asked you to come here, but this is—"

I pulled my hand away. "A bad time," I finished, unable to bear hearing Sweet Pea reject me for a fourth time this morning. "I get it. I guess I'll see you around the courthouse some time." I turned to walk back to the gate, but Sweet Pea stopped me, gently turning me to face him.

"Hold on, can we please start over?"

"I'm not sure," I said. "Believe it or not, it took a lot for me to come here today and—"

Before I could finish, Sweet Pea interrupted me with a kiss, and as much as I didn't want to, I pretty much melted into Sweet Pea's arms.

"That's not fair," I said.

"Come with me," he said, and walked me toward the building at the center of the compound.

"Clutch walked that way," I said. "Isn't church over there?"

Sweet Pea chuckled. "Church is about the last place on earth I'd take you. I'm taking you back to my room. You can hang out there while I finish up and then I'll come and get you."

"I'm supposed to hang out in your room until the coast is clear. What are we, teenagers?"

"I dunno. I never got to be one," he said innocently.

* * *

Taxi

"What now?" Trunk asked through the thick haze of celebratory cigar smoke that filled Wolf's office, or his 'den' as he liked to call it. With Char dead, and the coup a success, the Spiders' new President and Vice President had plans to make.

Wolf tilted his head back and exhaled slowly. "Now we do what Char should have. We go after the Burning Saints and anyone else who rides with them."

"Where do we start?"

"We're Spiders. So, we're gonna spin a web and catch us a fly."

"Got someone in mind, Boss?" I asked.

"As a matter of fact, I do," Wolf replied before turning to me. "You ready to earn your patch?"

I nodded.

"Good, because an unfamiliar face will be a big advantage for us."

"I'm squared away," I replied.

"You'd better be, because I'm taking a big fucking

chance using a guy I don't know. Especially on something like this." Wolf rose to his feet. "But you and Trunk served in Afghanistan together, and if he says you're solid, that's all I need to fucking know."

"He's more than solid," Trunk replied. "Believe it or not, this scrawny fuck saved my life."

"A decision I've regretted every day since," I said.

"You and me both," Wolf replied with a gruff chuckle, before turning serious again. "Look, it's simple. Do the job, and the patch is yours. Fail or try to fuck me over in any way..." Wolf smashed what remained of his cigar in the glass ashtray on top of his desk.

I nodded in understanding.

"I assume you want to hit Sweet Pea first?" Trunk asked.

"I'm gonna make that motherfucker suffer," Wolf replied. "I'm gonna rip him apart piece by piece until he begs for me to end his suffering."

"Which piece are you going to start with?" Trunk asked.

"His heart," Wolf sneered.

* * *

Sweet Pea

I stashed Callie in my room and bolted back to the chapel as quickly as possible. I felt bad for leaving her alone but didn't have any other option. It wasn't like I could let a new face roam the Sanctuary grounds, especially one as beautiful as Callie's. By the time I got back, the meeting was over, and Saints were filing out the door.

"What the fuck were you thinking inviting her here today?" Clutch snapped at me as I approached.

72

"I asked Callie to come here because I wanted her to meet the BFK guys before they rode out," I replied. "She's all about helping kids and I thought—"

"You thought you could score some 'nice guy' points with the smokin' hot lawyer," Clutch interrupted.

"Hey, fuck you," I snapped. "You were the one that was just bitching at me for not wanting to settle down, now I can't even bring a woman around without you chewing my ass?"

"A woman, Sweet Pea. As in, someone the club knows. Not a lawyer who works for the D.A.'s office, for Christ's sake. Minus and Cricket go way back, not to mention her brother rides with the Dogs. Eldie's been the club doctor for forever, and Devlin met your brother while working at Sally Anne's."

"What are you saying? I can only date women from some official club bachelorette list?"

"So, the two of you are dating now?"

"Goddamnit, Clutch. I don't know what the fuck we're doing and even if I did, I don't have to justify jack shit to you. I apologize for the timing of her showing up. That's on me and I'll straighten it out with Minus, but just because I report to you, doesn't mean you can tell me where to put my dick." I walked away, shoving Clutch aside with my shoulder as I did.

"We're not done talking about this!" Clutch called out as I increased the distance between us.

"Yes we fuckin' are," I replied, without looking back.

Minus was still in the Chapel when I entered. He was talking with Cowboy, Doozer, and Trouble.

"Hey, Pea. Everything okay?" Minus asked, a genuine look of concern on his face.

"Sorry, Minus, I didn't mean to interrupt. I just wanted to apologize for getting pulled out of church like that. It won't happen again," I said, turning to leave.

"It's okay, I'm glad you're here now. Was Doozer right? Were you meeting with a lawyer?"

"Yeah." I smiled, "But, she's just that. *A* lawyer, not *my* lawyer, like Doozer said before."

"Any reason she stopped by that I need to know about?"

"Well, actually," I said turning to Cowboy. "I was sort of hoping you'd have a few minutes to talk with her about a charity event before y'all take off," I said.

Minus smiled wide. "That's funny. Cowboy wanted to talk to you about leaving a little something behind. Someone actually."

"Who," I asked.

"Me," Trouble replied.

"Trouble feels like she's ready to put down roots, and I couldn't agree with her more," Cowboy said, with a hint of pride in his voice. "Given our transient nature, our club has always had an open-door policy with its club members."

"Seems your boy Doozer and Trouble here have grown somewhat attached and he wants to sponsor her," Minus added.

"As a Saints prospect?" I asked, turning to Doozer. "This is what you wanted to talk to me about earlier."

Doozer nodded.

"We need more soldiers. What do you think, Captain? Can you handle an addition to your crew?" Minus asked.

"She's tough, road-tested, and she can fix damned near anything," Cowboy said.

"Does *she* have anything to say about all of this?" I asked, looking directly at Trouble.

"If you're worried about me being a woman, don't," she said. "I may have a pussy, but that doesn't mean I am one."

I laughed, "Good enough for me." I then addressed her and Doozer together. "As far as you two hooking up, it's not a problem until it's a problem. If I find the two of you playing grab ass on the job, I'll take both your kuttes. You understand?"

"Yes, sir," Doozer said as he and Trouble nodded in unison.

I looked at Minus who nodded silently in approval.

"Good, then we'll let Trouble get her shit out of the trailer, and the rest of us gypsies can get back on the road."

Trouble and Doozer headed out excitedly and Cowboy shook Minus' hand. "You take good care of that one, okay? Her daddy died when she was just a pup, and step daddy did a number on her. She's tough as shit, and she's got a good heart, but she can be a tad on the impulsive side."

"How much is a tad exactly?"

"Less than you need, but more than you want," Cowboy said with a wink and a smile before turning to me. "Now, where's this lawyer you'd like me to meet?"

* * *

Callie

After mentally auditioning 'quaint,' 'minimalistic,' and 'cozy,' to describe my current surroundings I finally settled on *modest*. It was certainly better than 'shithole' and far cheerier than 'Guantanamo Bay prison cell.' I checked my watch. Sweet Pea left me in his room almost a half-hour ago and I was beginning to wonder how much longer I was to be confined in here.

Wait a minute. Am I a prisoner?

I got up and checked the doorknob, which turned

and opened with ease, making me feel foolish for thinking Sweet Pea would have locked me in. Or, was my lack of fear the craziest part about all of this? I was currently sitting in the clubhouse of a one-percent biker gang, which meant its members were willing to kill for their club. And although Sweet Pea had covered his patch, I had no idea what he was capable of. Still, though, I had a hard time imagining him harming me in any way.

I closed the door and sat back down on Sweet Pea's single bed. In addition to feeling foolish and confused, I was also starving. I skipped breakfast in order to wear this outfit comfortably, but now wished that I had snagged a chocolate glazed before Sweet Pea had handed the box of donuts over to Clutch. For now, I'd have to settle for whatever I found in Sweet Pea's mini fridge.

I opened the door to find three cans of beer, a half-empty jar of olives, and a bottle of expired antibiotics for a patient named "Stinky." I closed the door and huffed in defeat. So far, this morning had not gone at all as planned. In fact, nothing in my life seemed to be going as planned. Not the Knight case, not my career, and not even my impromptu date with Sweet Pea. I mean, good Lord, look where I was. Somehow, I'd managed to overcomplicate a one-night stand with a biker.

"What the hell are you doing here?" I asked out loud to no one.

Deciding the smartest move was to leave before things got weirder, and before I could complicate my life any further, I grabbed my purse and jacket and turned for the door just as Sweet Pea returned.

"You're not leaving, are you?" he asked, seeing I'd gathered my things.

"I probably should," I said.

"How come?" he asked so innocently it made me want to smack him directly in his big beautiful dumb face.

How come? How come? Maybe because you're a criminal and I'm sworn to uphold and protect the law. Or perhaps because in my lowest moment I tried to hire you to turn a man into hamburger because apparently, I've finally lost my mind.

"I have some things I need to take care of," I said calmly.

"Alright, but I'd really like you to meet Cowboy before you go," he said introducing me to the handsome biker standing behind him. He looked to be in his fifties, had salt and pepper hair, a handlebar moustache, and the patch on his vest read BFK PRESIDENT. "Callie Ames, Cowboy."

"It's very nice to meet you," I said and took Cowboy's well-weathered hand.

Cowboy held my hand but said nothing to me. He turned to Sweet Pea and asked, "Clutch is married to a doctor, isn't he?"

"Yeah. He sure is," Sweet Pea replied.

"She ever give you the once over?"

"As a matter of fact, Minus made the whole club get physicals last year."

"How'd you do on the eye test?"

"Just fine. Why do you ask?"

"Because you said you wanted to introduce me to a lawyer friend of yours, not a super model, and you clearly can't tell the difference."

"Alright, smooth talker, that's enough," Sweet Pea said, breaking up our handshake.

"Says, who?" I protested.

Cowboy and I chatted briefly about the charity gala and we exchanged contact information before he excused himself, leaving Sweet Pea and me alone in his room.

"Thank you for the introduction," I said. "Cowboy seems very sweet."

"He'd do anything for the kids, that's for sure."

"I admire his passion and hard work."

"I'd bet the two of you have a lot in common."

"Yup," I said, feeling awkwardness begin to creep in.

"So, I guess I'd better get going then,"

"Yeah, sure," Sweet Pea said, rubbing the back of his neck. "Do you need a ride anywhere?"

"No, I drove here."

"Oh, okay." Sweet Pea shuffled his feet.

"I'm kind of starving so I'm gonna grab something to eat and head back to my apartment."

"We have a full kitchen here. I could whip something up for you right now if you'd like."

Of course, he can cook.

"No, that's okay. I—"

"Or we could go someplace together."

A short, involuntary laugh escaped before I could stop it.

"What?" Sweet Pea asked, innocently.

"What do you mean *what*?"

"You must be deadly during cross examination," he said smiling wide, which was super fucking annoying as I found it impossible to remain in an agitated state while looking at his dimples.

"I appreciate the introduction to Cowboy, but this morning has otherwise been a total disaster. You invited me here and then had to be convinced by Clutch to let me through the gate."

"Callie, I didn't mean to—"

"Nope. You're not going to charm your way out of

this," I snapped. "I don't know what kind of women you're used to dealing with, but I'm not the kind to be shoved in a closet while you run off and play cowboys and assholes with your friends."

Sweet Pea's smile widened, broken only when he leaned down and kissed me. A kiss that was not only unlike any that I'd received from him before, but unlike any kiss I'd ever experienced. One hand went to my face, his thumb gently stroking my cheek as he held me tight against him.

"I'm sorry," he said, breaking our kiss. "I just wasn't expecting you."

"But last night you said—"

"I don't mean today, Callie. I wasn't expecting you in my life." He stepped back and motioned around him. "As you can probably tell, I'm kind of a solitary guy. My life is simple. I do what the club needs, I work out, I watch a little SportsCenter, and when I need company, I find it."

"You mean when you need to get laid, you know women that are happy to accommodate," I said.

"If that's the way you want to put it, sure. But my private life never bleeds into my club life. In fact, I've never brought a woman to my room before."

"I can't for the life of me see why not. It's so… charming."

"It's a rathole and that's the way I want it," he said matter-of-factly. "In order to do what I do well, I need to stay on edge. If I get too comfortable, that edge gets dull. Plus, my life doesn't easily lend itself to settling down."

"So, because relationships aren't easy for you, they're off the table?" I asked.

Sweet Pea took a moment to process my question before responding. "It's more like, the idea of a relationship has never been on my table before." Sweet Pea took my hands in his. "I'm not being dramatic when I say my life is crazy."

"I think I have a better understanding of your *lifestyle* than most," I said.

"Last year my lifestyle, as you put it, surpassed crazy and graduated to utter chaos. Now, that chaos is about to be thrown into a blender, and I have no idea what things are gonna look like after that."

"Why are you telling me all of this?"

"I dunno. Because I can, I guess," he said softly. "You wouldn't know this, but I don't typically get so chummy with people I've just met."

"Chummy?" I laughed. "Is that what we are? Chums?"

"Works for me. All I know is, for whatever reason I find it easy to talk to you, and that's not normal for me."

"I have to be honest, I don't see a whole lot of 'normal' in your life."

"Maybe not, but what the fuck is normal, anyway? Is your life normal? It seems to me like you're just as alone as I am. Maybe your cave downtown is nicer than mine here, but at least mine is free of snakes."

"Point taken, but I think our list of similarities ends at solitary 'creatures.'"

"Maybe, maybe not, but I'd like to find out. Lemme make sure everything is squared away here, and then I'll take you out to lunch."

"I *am* starving," I admitted.

"I would have polished off those leftovers from Sally Anne's for breakfast," Sweet Pea said.

"I probably would have, too, if I hadn't left the bag in the back seat of my Uber."

"Best tip that lucky sonofabitch got all night."

It wasn't the best one I got last night.

NINE

BURNING SAINTS

Callie

IT HAD BEEN two days since I'd seen Sweet Pea, but he'd managed to infiltrate just about every thought I'd had since then. As much as I hated to admit it, he was a welcome distraction to my shit storm of a career and the train wreck of my personal life. But as fun a distraction as he was, and sweet Jesus was he, I was frightened by how quickly a biker had gotten under my skin.

My phone buzzed, and my heart raced at the thought of a text from Sweet Pea, which made me feel foolish. Not that I had anything to worry about, as it wasn't a text from Sweet Pea, but a call from my father.

"Hello, Dad," I said, trying to sound 'neutrally cheery.'

"Callie, what's wrong?" My dad's uncanny power to see right through my bullshit on full display.

"What? Who said anything was wrong?"

"After the Knight verdict, I expected the usual call from you. It's been close to a week now and still no call."

"It's been four days, and everything is okay. I'm sorry I didn't call you I've just been...busy."

"Too busy for a call?"

Yes, father. I've been busy. First, I was busy plotting the kidnap and torture of a man I failed to put in prison. Then I got distracted when a giant Norseman used my stump to throw his axe into... repeatedly. But lately I've been busy crying on my sofa while watching my only friend eat rats.

"The law never sleeps. You know that, Dad."

"Come on, Callie. Give me a little credit, will ya? You think I don't know you a little better than that?"

"I'm sorry I didn't call. I really am. I've never missed one of our post-trial debriefings and I shouldn't have missed this one. Especially this one." Tears began to form and my voice waivered.

"You wanna talk about it, Sharkey?"

"Thanks, Dad, but I really am okay."

"Really?"

"No." I laughed through my tears. "But I'm trying."

"You call me or come to the house any time you need me. You hear me?"

"If only all those hardened criminals you've put away over the years knew what a softy you really are."

"You tell them, and I'll show them the photo album of you during the head gear years."

"You wouldn't dare."

"Robo-Sharkey 2000."

"I take it back. You're a mean old man."

"That's my girl."

"I love you, Dad."

"I love you too, Sharkey. Let's do dinner at the house soon, okay?"

"Okay, that sounds nice. Bye, Daddy."

I hung up and went back to what I was doing previously. Staring at the stack of briefs on my desk that I desperately wanted to 'wish away into the cornfield.'

My phone buzzed again, and I summoned my energy for round number two with my well-meaning but sometimes emotionally draining father. However, this time it actually was a text from Sweet Pea and he wasted no time getting right down to business.

Sweet Pea: *Hey, Counselor. You free tonight?*

I resisted the urge to instantly type back YES and instead played it cool.

Me: *New phone. Who dis?*

Sweet Pea: *Remember when I said you were funny? I'd like that stricken from the record please.*

Me: *Too late. No takebacks.*

Sweet Pea: *I'm not sure you went to real law school.*

Me: *Where to?*

Sweet Pea: *How am I supposed to know where you attended fake law school?*

Me: *No. Where to, as in where are you taking me tonight?*

Sweet Pea: *A victory party.*

Of all the answers I may have expected, that wasn't one of them.

Me: Victory party? Did someone win an election?

Sweet Pea: *Just think of it as a big family dinner.*

83

Me: *Sure, if you think I'd be welcome.*
Sweet Pea: *Pick you up at your place at 8:00?*
Me: *On your bike?!?!*
Sweet Pea: *I have a car. Dress casual. See you at 8:00.*

* * *

Rob walked into my office just as I was finishing my text conversation with Sweet Pea.

"You busy?" he asked. "I need a second set of eyeballs on this settlement agreement before going into arbitration tomorrow morning."

"I'm free. Just avoiding work," I replied.

"Who are you texting?" he asked, spying my phone.

"Nosy," I said, pulling it to my chest.

"It's him, isn't it?"

"Who?" I asked, unconvincingly.

"It is. You're texting with Kimble."

"He doesn't like to be called that." My hand shot to my mouth.

"I knew it," Rob said, and I prepared myself for an epic battle with my buttoned-up colleague. Rob carefully removed the stack of papers from the chair in front of my desk and sat down. "Tell me everything," he said, excitedly.

"What?" I asked, completely shocked by his reaction.

"I could tell when you walked in yesterday that something was up with you," he said smiling. "Wait a minute." Rob shut my office door and whispered, "You did it with him, didn't you?"

"What?"

"You did," he repeated. "You actually had sex with that hot biker."

"What the hell?" I sputtered. "I thought you were going to be upset with me."

"I was scared to death at first, but by the sound of your texts that night, it sounded like you were having a really good time. Once I knew you were safe, I was able to relax."

"I'm sorry, I'm still confused."

"Why?"

"I guess I thought you might also be a little upset because maybe you had a...thing for me."

Rob stared at me silently before bursting out into a fit of laughter.

"Gee, thanks for the confidence booster," I said.

"Callie, I'm gay," Rob said, tears of laughter streaming down his face.

"Oh, my God. I'm an idiot," I said, stunned.

"I'm sorry. I guess we've never talked about it before. I just assumed you always knew."

"Rob, the only thing worse than my ability to tell when someone is into me or not, is my gaydar. Plus, I always catch you staring at me."

"Of course, I stare at you. You're gorgeous. Sorry to burst your bubble, but I'd rather be like you than *with* you, Callie."

I laughed.

"Now that I've shared, you'd better spill the beans about the biker."

I told Rob every detail from top to bottom, except the bits about me losing my mind, and it honestly felt good to talk to someone.

"Whose party are you going to tonight?"

"That's a good question, I never asked. He said it was a *victory* party."

"How does one dress for a victory party? I guess it doesn't really matter, right? It's not like you know any of his friends anyway," Rob said.

"That's true. Plus, no matter who it is, I'm bringing the same gift I bring everyone on every occasion."

"You can never go wrong with good booze."

"It's the gift that keeps on giving," I smiled.

* * *

Sweet Pea picked me up right on time and I licked my lips as soon as I opened the door. Lordy, the man was a walking monument to the Nordic gene pool. "Hi," I breathed out.

"Jesus Christ, Callie. What the fuck are you wearing?" he asked, walking inside and closing the door.

I glanced down my body and shrugged. I wore my Jimmy Choo lace up boots, a leather mini skirt and a Harley-Davidson T-shirt I'd cut up to give it a more 'biker' chic feel. "You said casual. Is it too casual? Do I look bad?"

"No, baby, the problem is you look fuckin' edible."

I smiled. "I want to make a good impression on your friends."

"The only good impression you should care about is mine."

I grabbed my bag, dropping my keys inside. "Oh, I took care of that as well."

"Yeah?"

Nodding, I reached up and tugged gently on his beard. "I'm not wearing panties."

He let out a quiet hiss. "Are you fucking kidding me?"

"I'd never kid about panties, Pea."

Before I could fully register what he was doing, my purse was removed from my hands and dropped on the floor, and my skirt was slid up my thighs.

"Fuck," he rasped, as he knelt in front of me, pressing his face between my legs.

I gripped his shoulders for balance. "What are you doing, you maniac? We need to go."

"We've got time." He ran his tongue over my clit, sliding one hand between my thighs. "Spread, Callie."

I spread a little more and he pressed two fingers inside of me, his thumb tapping my clit as his fingers moved. Before I could come, however, he pulled out and stood.

"What are you doing?" I growled.

He grinned, unbuttoning his jeans. "You feel like gettin' bendy?"

"I love bendy." I bit my lip and grinned. "Bendy's my favorite."

"Sofa," he ordered, and I made my way to the sofa and bent over the arm.

He gently kicked my legs apart and he squeezed my ass. "Did I tell you not to wear panties, Callie?"

"No."

His hand landed on my right cheek with a loud slap. "What happens when you do things like that without permission?"

"Hopefully, equal amounts of ass slappery," I sassed.

I was rewarded with my left cheek being smacked and I felt my pussy contract with need. I raised a hand to reach for him, but he smacked me again.

"Did I say you could move?" he challenged. "Grip the armrest, Callie."

His hand pressed against my mound and he gave me a gentle tap. "Soaked."

I hummed in response.

"Tonight," he whispered, slipping two fingers inside me again, "this is mine for the taking whenever I so desire. You will be open to me, literally, all night."

"I—"

"You set the tone, Callie, when you chose to go bare, so you'll obey me in this."

"I wasn't going to argue," I said, unable to stop a grin.

"Like that you're a fast learner, baby." He spread me slightly, rolled on a condom, then slid his cock inside of me. "This is gonna be quick."

"You can make it quick, but make my ass red, okay?" I begged.

"Jesus," he hissed, slamming into me, but honoring my request by palming my ass in time with his hips.

"Now, Pea," I cried as an orgasm washed over me, squeezing the sofa arm as ecstasy swamped me. "Oh, god."

He continued to thrust, then he grunted, his body covering me, his hands landing on each side of mine as his dick pulsed inside of me. "You better pack some baby wipes," he warned.

I licked my lips and nodded. "I should probably pack some panties, too, huh?"

That earned me a smack on my ass and I grinned. "I won't wear them, I promise. I'll have them just in case."

"I'll allow it." He pulled out of me and walked toward my bathroom. "Don't move."

He returned with a warm washcloth and cleaned me up, then slid my skirt back down and turned me to face him, kissing me gently. "You look beautiful, baby."

"You could have led with that."

He chuckled. "You threw me with the no panties business."

"Next time I'll wait for you to tell me I'm beautiful, *then* throw you with the 'no panties business,'" I promised, and slid my hand between his legs, cupping him over his jeans. "I want a chance to taste you tonight, okay?"

He grinned, leaning down to kiss me. "Yeah, baby, I can make that happen."

* * *

Sweet Pea

My dick was still hard as we left for the party, and I had to resist the urge to take her back inside and fuck her ten ways from Sunday.

I was not prepared for her to be 'up' for play, and I was beginning to see there were layers to Callie Ames that I looked forward to peeling away.

"Oh my god, you own an R8 coupe?" she breathed out and I raised an eyebrow.

"I do. Do you like it?" I asked, holding the passenger side door for her.

"I love it. Audi makes an incredible car."

"That they do," I agreed and closed her in, jogging to the driver's side and sliding in beside her.

"So, what should I expect tonight?"

"Given your good taste in cars and men, I think you'll have a good time."

"I'm used to stuffy, lawyer-filled cocktail parties that I can't wait to leave the moment I arrive.

"There will be lots of alcohol, probably some public displays of debauchery. You never know at a club party."

"Right." She grinned. "So, the booze I bought should go over well."

"It's booze," I said. "Booze always goes over well."

We headed to the Sanctuary and pulled into a space near the front. I helped her out, making sure I slid my hand between her legs for a brief second and smiled when I heard her quiet gasp.

"You're gonna make tonight impossible, aren't you?" she deduced.

I chuckled. "Only if you're lucky."

"Oh, wait. I forgot to ask. Whose victory are we celebrating?"

"Clutch and Eldie's, son," I replied. "He's a young boxing phenom, and he just won big fight."

"Clutch? Oh, my God. He won't want me here."

"Why would you say that?"

"He didn't seem very happy about my presence here the other day."

"Clutch is a good guy, he's just a professional asshole. He's been riding me pretty hard since getting my Road Captain's patch, but I think he's just trying to look out for me. Don't worry about him. He'll like you just fine."

"If you say so."

"Besides, my brother is the one you really have to worry about," I said.

"Wait, what?" Callie replied in a panicked tone, but I took her hand and guided her inside to find the party already in full swing.

"Sweet Pea!" Minus bellowed with a laugh. "You're late!"

I grinned. "No, I'm not."

"Ignore him," Cricket, his woman, suggested as she walked over to us. "He's already an entire sheet to the wind." She stuck her hand out with a grin. "I'm Cricket. Minus is mine. Well, when I choose to claim him."

Callie shook her hand with a laugh. "I'm Callie. It's nice to meet you."

"Come on in. I'll introduce you to a few people."

"I can do that, babe," I said, not wanting Callie out of my sight.

Cricket raised an eyebrow. "But then I can't talk

about you behind your back."

"I brought a gift," Callie said, raising the bottle. "It's alcohol. I just found out this is a party for a child, so now I feel like an idiot."

"Screw the kids. This'll be for us adults," Cricket said. "Follow me to the gift table."

Cricket expertly separated my woman from me and led her over to where gifts were already overloading a table, and I watched them closely as they chatted.

"So, I see you're represented by legal counsel this evening," Clutch joked beside me.

I gave him a side glance before focusing back on Callie. "Yeah."

"Are you domesticatin' after all?"

"If you like the idea of settling down so much, how about you marry yourself? Then, you can take off on a honeymoon where you can go fuck yourself."

He laughed, shaking his head. "Sorry, but I'm just not my type. Come on, I'll buy you a drink."

We headed to the bar where Warthog was pouring drinks and offering gummy bears from a silver tray.

"The green, yellow, and red ones are great, but the orange ones will take you to the moon," he said, wide-eyed.

I opted for a beer instead, then had him pour a double bourbon for Callie and went to find her. She was in a deep conversation with Cricket, Eldie, and Devlin.

Fuck.

I needed to break up that little hen party right quick.

"I need to know where you got those boots," Eldie said. I totally want a pair."

"They're about five years old," Callie said. "I don't know if you can find them anymore, but I'll give you all the deets just in case."

"Thanks." Eldie caught my eye and smiled. "Hey,

Pea."

I leaned down and kissed her cheek. "Hey, babe. Congratulations."

"Thanks, honey. I suppose I should go find my man, huh?"

As the women went to find their men, I wrapped an arm around Callie and handed her the bourbon, which she sipped, then let out the sexiest sigh on the planet.

"Careful," I warned.

She smiled up at me and ran her tongue over her top lip. "Or what?"

I glanced around the room, saw that everyone's focus was on other things, so I guided Callie into the small office used by most of us when we needed a private place to do business.

Taking her glass from her, I set it on the desk, turning her to face it and sliding her skirt up over her ass. I slid my foot between her feet and kicked them apart. "Spread."

"Did you lock the door?" she rasped.

"No."

"What if someone comes in?"

"Then they'll see me fucking you and know you belong to me."

She spread her legs while I unbuttoned my jeans, pushing them down far enough for my dick to have free range, before rolling on a condom, then I buried myself deep inside of her. Jesus, her tight, wet pussy was almost too much to take. "Fuck," I breathed out.

"Oh, my god, Pea, I'm gonna come," she panted out as I slammed into her, the only sound was our breathing and flesh slapping flesh.

"Wait," I ordered.

"I can't."

I pulled out and she whimpered with need. "What

are you doing?"

"I'm giving you a minute to take a breath."

She scowled at me over her shoulder. "Fuck that," she said, slipping her hand between her legs and going to fucking town on her clit with her fingers.

I almost came watching her, but deciding I wanted her cum on my dick, I slammed back inside of her and thrust hard over and over until her pussy clamped down and milked every bit of me.

"Jesus," I hissed.

"Yes, that," she whispered.

I pulled out of her, cleaned up as best I could with the baby wipes in her purse, then helped her get herself together.

"Tomorrow, I want to show you something."

She raised an eyebrow. "What more could you possibly show me?"

"Got a few things up my sleeve." I grinned. "But for now, let's head back to the party."

"I want more of that bourbon."

"I could also hook you up with our very own Willy Wonka if you like gummy bears," I said, and took her back out to the great room.

TEN

BURNING SAINTS

Callie

SWEET PEA HANDED me another glass of bourbon and I smiled up at him as I took a sip. He ran his finger over my mouth, then leaned down to kiss me, his tongue sweeping against the seam of my lips. "Tasty."

I nodded. "It's good right?"

"Kinda want to lick it off your body next time I fuck you."

"You're insatiable," I said, smacking his chest playfully.

"You started this, just remember that."

"How do you figure? You walked up to me at the

courthouse."

"Bullshit," Sweet Pea said. "I walked *by* you. We made eye contact and you were on me like white on rice."

"That couldn't possibly be true, and I can prove it," I said.

"How?"

"I hate rice."

"*Hate rice?*" He laughed. "How can anyone hate rice?"

"*The Lost Boys*," I said.

"The 80's movie?"

"Yes. Remember the scene where the gang is eating Chinese food at the hideout, and Kiefer Southerland passes Jason Patric the rice?"

"Their characters' names were David and Michael," Sweet Pea replied, matter-of-factly.

"You and I clearly watched the movie for different reasons," I said.

"At least we finally have something in common," Sweet Pea smiled. "A love of 80's horror movies."

"*Well...*" I screwed up my face and shrugged.

"You're kidding," Sweet Pea said deflated. "You don't like horror?"

"I was pretty sheltered growing up. The only reason I saw *The Lost Boys* in the first place was because I was at a slumber party where everyone was watching it. My friends and I were all obsessed with hot actors from back in the 80's and everybody was talking about the guys in *The Lost Boys*. I'd never seen a horror movie before, and it pretty much scarred me for life."

"First of all, *The Lost Boys* is barely a horror movie, and you've really never seen *Halloween* or *Friday the 13th*?"

"Which one of those has Freddy in it?" I asked.

"Neither," he said, exasperated. "That's *A Nightmare on Elm Street.* Freddy's the guy with the blades on his glove."

"I thought that was *Edward Scissorhands*," I said.

"Jesus Herbert Kristofferson," Sweet Pea said.

"Anyway," I said, trying to get my tipsy little thought train back on track. "*Lost Boys,* Chinese food..."

"Of course, I remember the scene," Sweet Pea continued. "David makes the noodles look like worms and the rice look like—"

"Don't finish that sentence!" I shouted, my hand covering his mouth. "Don't you dare say that word."

"What?" he asked through the narrow gaps between my fingers.

"The *M* word," I replied in a whisper.

Sweet Pea nodded in agreement and I removed my hand.

"When did you first see *The Lost Boys*?" he asked, matching my hushed tone.

"I was thirteen."

"And you've haven't eaten rice since?"

"Can't even have it on my plate," I replied.

"Have any issues with it before the film?"

"Nope."

"Thank you for sharing that story with me, Callie, I've really learned something important about you tonight."

"The fact that I can't stand the sight of rice because of a cheesy vampire movie is important?"

"No. Tonight I learned you are an insane person."

Sweet Pea smiled and I felt myself sink one level deeper into an intense emotional connection with him. A man I barely knew and had nothing in common with had gotten my attention in every way and if I wasn't careful,

I was going to get myself into deep trouble. I was already acting completely irresponsibly with my career by entering a consensual sexual relationship with a member of a known criminal organization. I heard a combination of my father's voice and every law professor I ever had ringing through my head, but the truth was, their words weren't reaching my heart at all.

"Hey," Sweet Pea said, pulling me back. "I want to show you something." He led me to the other side of the great room, stopping at an ornately carved oak door which was locked by an electronic keypad.

"I think you've shown me quite enough tonight, mister," I said as Sweet Pea punched in the code before leading me through the doorway.

Boy, was I wrong.

"We don't normally let non-members in here, but I wanted to show you my favorite part of the Sanctuary."

"Sweet Pea. It's beautiful," I said.

"We call this the Holy of Holies. It's a monument to all the Saints that have passed."

The large space was lined with lighted glass cabinets, each one filled with helmets, patches, jewelry, and various other biker's totems. There were at least a dozen motorcycles from various eras proudly on display. The entire space was lit like a museum that was curated with love and deep affection. It was a profoundly moving thing to see and I felt honored Sweet Pea had shown it to me.

I grabbed the sides of Sweet Pea's face and kissed him deeper than I'd ever kissed a man. My desire to not only be with him, but somehow be a part of him, caused my insides to burn. At that moment, I felt closer and more connected to Sweet Pea than ever before. Even when we were having sex. And that was the best sex I'd ever had.

"What was that?" Sweet Pea asked, clearly as shocked by the moment as I was.

"Can I be one hundred percent honest with you?" I asked, terrified he'd say yes.

"Yes."

I looked to Sweet Pea's eyes, my arms around his neck, and said, "I have no idea why I'm here."

"Aw. You know just what to say to a guy," he replied with a smile and gave me a kiss.

"I'm serious. I'm a family lawyer with the D.A.'s office and you're..."

"An ex-criminal biker," Sweet Pea completed my sentence.

"To put it nicely, yes. My association with you could get me into some hot water. Possibly even disbarred."

"So why *are* you here? Why take the risk?"

"I think maybe I'm rebelling," I replied.

"Rebelling against who?"

"Whom," I corrected. "I've been thinking a lot about that lately, and I think it's not so much a whom as it is a what."

"Look, if you've got some kind of Abbot and Costello routine worked out here, I'd rather take you back to the bedroom."

"Stop it, I'm being serious."

"I'm sorry, go on."

"I've been unhappy at my job for a while and losing the Knight case, or more importantly how poorly I handled it, has really shown me exactly how unhappy. I want to leave the D.A.'s office, but I'm not sure what to do next, and that terrifies me. I'm used to a certain degree of control in my life, and I think I've been using you to distract me from the fact that things are very much out of control."

Sweet Pea put his dimples on full display and took

my chin in his hand.

"I'm happy to be your distraction and even happier to know we really do have a lot in common."

"Really?"

"You have no idea."

* * *

Sweet Pea

"Let's just say, I relate to you about being a control freak," I said sitting us down on the leather sofa next to Red Dog's custom Harley Bobber.

"I never said *freak*," Callie protested.

"Okay, how about positive outcome enthusiast?"

"I like that a lot better," she said with a smile. "But I wouldn't have pegged you as a member of the club. You always seem so relaxed."

"That's the idea," I said.

"So, you're saying this is all an act?"

"No. Not an act. More like armor. If I act like shit can't get to me, shit doesn't tend to get to me, that's all."

"Why do men always make everything sound so simple?"

"I never said I speak for all men, hell I doubt I even speak for most men, but I do think most things in life tend to be simpler than we allow them to be."

"Such as?"

"Sex, for one."

"Here we go again." Callie rolled her eyes. "Can you stop trying to get me back in there?" she asked, motioning in the direction of the boardroom.

"I object, Your Honor. The prosecution is attempting to prejudice the jury."

Callie cocked her head and smiled in surprise. "Objection sustained. You may continue your argument."

"All I said was people overcomplicate sex. If two consenting adults want to have sex and aren't morally bound to be monogamous, then they should be able to knock boots without anyone getting in their business."

"So, you 'knock boots' with a lot of women, then?"

"Leading the witness, your honor."

"I'm impressed, counselor."

"I told you I attend a lot of hearings."

"Why is that?" Callie asked.

"It started when I first got to Portland. My brother would be busy with club business and I'd be all alone for hours. I was completely broke and wasn't even old enough to drive, so to pass the time, I'd take the bus down to the courthouse and attend hearings. Small cases, big cases, I didn't really care, I just loved being there. I've been doing it ever since."

"Libraries and parks are free too. Why not hang out there?"

"Believe me. I'd hang out wherever I could until someone would tell me to fuck off. I guess no one ever did at the courthouse, not that it would have mattered. By then I was pretty hooked."

"What possessed you to watch all those hearings, do you think?"

"I don't know, really. If I had to put it into words, I guess something inside of me wants to see the scales of justice balanced. I kind of go into a blind rage when I see people being victimized."

"Is that why you became an enforcer?" Callie asked quickly, before taking a sip from her glass.

"You trying to show me up? I throw out a few legal terms, so you go biker on me?" I teased.

"Well?"

"Yeah, I guess. Without going into too much detail,

my job in the club was to protect the people who paid us to keep them and their property safe. I was good at it, but now I'm a Road Captain and the club is out of that line of work."

"Have you ever thought about becoming a lawyer?"

"Are you serious?" I asked, unable to tell if she was busting my balls.

"Why not? You seem to have a real passion and interest in the law."

"Been pretty good at breaking it too, and law schools tend to frown on that kinda shit."

"You don't have to go to law school to take the bar exam," Callie said.

"Really?"

"Really," she said.

"There is still an ethics review, though, and a criminal record would definitely show up on that."

"Hmmm," Callie replied.

"I guess I'll just have to settle for our little mock trial," I said leaning in for a kiss.

"Wait," Callie interrupted. "You didn't answer my first question."

"About what?"

"Just how many women have you taken to your chambers?"

"Is my client still under oath?" I asked.

"You know what they say about lawyers who represent themselves, right?"

"Other than they're always guilty as sin and crazier than shit house rats? Besides, we were talking about you wanting to quit your job, not about me."

"I propose a change of venue as well as a change of topic. I don't want to talk or think about work anymore tonight," Callie said, standing up. "You were right. Keep life simple. This is a party and I want to meet the rest or your club, so let's go mingle."

"If we have to," I grumbled.

"Are you trying to hide me from everyone or one person in particular?"

I laughed. "Not much gets by you, does it?"

"You've been pulling me into one private spot or another all night long. I fear we'll either be talking or fucking in a coat closet before too long if I don't drag you out of here."

"I'm not trying to hide you," I argued. "I'm just trying not to...cross the streams."

"Cross the streams?"

"It's a *Ghostbusters* reference. You did see it, right? Or did the fact that 'ghost' was in the title make it too scary for you?"

Callie blushed. "Stop making fun of me. Of course, I've seen *Ghostbusters*."

"Then you remember crossing the streams is bad."

"Your club is one stream and I'm another, and you're afraid combining us will cause problems."

"That's right."

"Then why invite me here tonight?"

"Because maybe crossing the streams isn't bad. I don't know," I groaned out, frustrated that I couldn't find the right words to convey how I felt. "I want you here, Callie. I promise. I guess I also want you all to myself. I like whatever it is we have going on between us, and I don't want my club life fucking it up. That probably doesn't make any sense."

Callie leaned in and kissed me softly. "I think we have one more thing in common," she said.

"What's that?"

"We both suck at dating," she smiled.

"You might be right," I said. "So, we won't call it dating. We're just..."

"Chums," Callie replied.

I chuckled. "Yes, chums."

* * *

Callie

I licked my lips, shifting so I could straddle him. "How about we get chummy now?"

Sweet Pea gripped my hips, then slid my skirt up my thighs. "You wanna get chummy in the holy of holies?"

I leaned down and kissed him gently. "Hell, yes, I do. Something to add to your good memories."

He grinned, sliding his hand between my legs and thumbing my clit as he kissed my neck. "I want your tits out, baby. Keep your bra on, but show me everything else."

I lifted my T-shirt, pulling the cups of my bra down, my nipples already hard enough to cut glass, while he released his dick.

"Changed my mind," I said.

"What?"

"I want to taste you."

I slid off his lap and knelt between his legs, wrapping my hand around his girth and licking the precum off the tip of his cock. "God, you taste amazing."

He stroked my cheek and smiled, and I slid my lips over the tip, sucking gently as I moved my hand down his length. Sweet Pea shifted slightly and I was forced to take him deeper, which suited me just fine. Then he began to fuck my face and I groaned as my pussy screamed for release.

As I sucked him, one hand working him along with my mouth, I slipped my free hand between my legs and writhed against my fingers as he buried himself in my mouth. My eyes watered as his sheer size nearly choked me, but I couldn't stop. I was soaked and I slid my fingers inside of me, then slapped at my pussy, before working my clit, then slapping again.

"Now, Callie," he warned, and I slid my fingers deep inside of me as his cum shot down my throat. I took every ounce, sucking until I'd milked him dry.

As I sat back, Sweet Pea pulled my hand away from my pussy, licking my fingers clean before helping me stand on wobbly legs, and bending me over the sofa.

His hand landed with loud smack on my ass, and I heard the tear of foil before his dick thrust inside of me. How the hell he got hard again so quickly, I had no idea, but I wasn't about to complain.

"Did I give you permission to suck me off?" he demanded, his hand landing on my ass again.

"No," I rasped, his cock thrusting deeper.

"What happens when you don't ask permission, Callie?"

I licked my lips pushing back against him. "I get punished. I hope."

"You got wipes in your purse, right?"

"Yes," I whispered.

"You happen to bring lube?"

"Jesus," I rasped. "Yes."

"Shit, seriously?"

"Yeah. I'm a fucking Girl Scout. Always prepared."

"Get it," he demanded, slapping my ass.

I reached for my bag, unzipping it and grabbing the tube, handing it back to him.

"Do not move," he demanded.

I heard the snap of the cap, then he pulled out of me and I felt every inch of him leave my body, unable to stop a whimper.

The thud of the lube falling on a sofa cushion was the only noise in the room as Sweet Pea ran a finger over my tight hole. "You ready for me to play here?"

"Yes," I hissed, and his dick was inside of me. The lube and the condom made it extra slick and surprisingly, not painful. Slowly, he pushed further in until I was sure I'd lose my mind.

"You okay?" he asked, sliding deeper.

"Yes," I rasped, my hands gripping the arm of the sofa.

"More?"

"Jesus. Yes!" I demanded, and he obliged.

"Spread, Callie."

I spread, and he inched further in, reaching between us and sliding his fingers inside my pussy as he fucked my ass. I cried out as overload hit my body, my breasts heavy, and my clit aching with need. As his fingers fucked my pussy and his dick fucked my ass, I slid my fingers to my clit, slapping and pushing against it.

"I can't wait, Pea," I panted out.

"You don't come until I tell you," he said.

"Pea, please," I begged.

He slapped my ass, and I cried out, the sensation almost too much to bear. "Wait, Callie."

He pulled his fingers from my pussy, slapping his fingers against my mound as he thrust twice more and then I felt his dick pulse and I whimpered.

"Come," he whispered, and I let my body go.

Sweet Pea pulled out slowly, gently, then lifted me, sitting on the sofa and holding me tight against his body. "So fuckin' good, baby."

My body was so wrecked, I almost cried. His jeans were still at his ankles, my skirt was still up around my waist with my tits out as he held me close. I didn't care. I burrowed my face against his neck and kissed his pulse.

"Did that hurt?" he asked.

"Not even a little bit," I said. "I don't know how I'm going to feel tomorrow, but I don't actually care."

"You're the absolute perfect... chum."

I chuckled. "Don't ever forget it."

I don't know how long we sat there, but no one bothered us, so we stayed in a state of satiation I'd certainly never experienced before. After a while, though, it was time to get back to the party, so with Sweet Pea's promise that this would most definitely happen again, we cleaned up and headed back to his friends.

ELEVEN

BURNING SAINTS

Callie

I FOLLOWED SWEET Pea to a condo building in the Pearl and couldn't stop a frown of confusion as we pulled into an underground parking garage. It had been a week of "chumming" around with Sweet Pea whenever we were both free, but it was always at my apartment. Today he surprised me by telling me he wanted to take me to his place for some fun.

Sweet Pea pulled his bike into a parking space and nodded to the one next to it, so I parked there and rolled down my window. "You live here?"

He grinned, removing his helmet and leaning inside my car. "Sort of. Come on. I'll explain."

I climbed out of my car and took the hand he held out, then let him lead me to the bank of elevators to the right of our vehicles. We rode up...and up...stopping at the sixteenth floor and he guided me out and to the left. Unlocking the door at the end of the hallway, he stepped back so I could precede him, and I walked inside to total, complete, and utter opulence. "Wow," I whispered.

The foyer opened to the great room, where floor to ceiling windows overlooked the Willamette River, and a massive island separated the living room from the kitchen. There was a staircase off to the right and a hallway that led to a bathroom, office, and bedroom.

"I can't even imagine what rent in a place like this would be," I breathed out.

"I own it," Sweet Pea said, disappearing into the kitchen.

Right, Kimble money. Of course he owned the building.

"It's gorgeous," I said.

"I have something for you," Sweet Pea said, returning with a square white box with a bright red bow on top.

"You got me a present?" I asked.

"It's for Ruby, actually," he said.

I opened the box to find two feeder mice in a plastic carrier.

"An apology gift for being so rude to her when we first met," he said, with a smile, his dimples on full display.

I never wanted to fuck a man more than I wanted to fuck Sweet Pea at that moment.

"And now you're wondering why the fuck I keep a room at the Sanctuary, right?"

I tried to soften my expression, but he was right. "Sort of?"

He smiled. "Look, I keep my private life as separate as I can from my club life. If we're gonna start something, you need to know exactly what you're in for."

"Okay." I swallowed. "Are you going to tell me you fuck hard and then lead me to your red room of pain?"

"It's not red."

I took a deep breath. "You have a sex dungeon?"

Sweet Pea chuckled. "Not a dungeon. I think it would be easier to show you." He cupped my cheek. "Do you trust me?"

I nodded.

"Are you scared?"

"No."

And I wasn't. Yes, he was a giant. Yes, he could kill a man with his bare hands, but he'd been nothing but gentle with me, and I trusted him. Maybe a little more than I should, but I often went with my gut and when I did, it never led me astray.

He took my hand and led me up the stairs, pushing open a door right at the top, and flipping on the light. He was right, the room wasn't red. It was white. Well, other than one wall which was a dark blue. It was actually quite pretty. A king-sized bed sat under the window and he had built-in cabinets surrounding the room, all white.

It looked incredibly...benign.

Well, it did until he started pushing buttons on the side of the built-ins and drawers popped open with all manner of sex toys, handcuffs, whips, etcetera, etcetera.

"Okay, so how fucked up are you?" I asked.

"Less than fifty shades, probably more than thirty," he retorted.

I faced him. "Are you, like, needing multiple partners? Swinging, that kind of thing?"

"No. When I'm in a partnership, it's just with that person for as long as we both decide."

"Are you the submissive?" He raised an eyebrow and I chuckled. "I just thought I'd put it out there."

"I like the control, but I'm not about subjecting pain."

"Why?"

"Not ready to go there with you, Callie."

"But there's a reason."

"Isn't there always?"

I sighed. "I guess so. Am I going to have to sign a contract?"

"No. We don't even need to have a safe word... I mean, unless you want one. You've already proved you can a lot, but you just say stop and we stop."

"Yeah, about that..."

"What?"

"I've never, ah, taken it up the ass before," I said, blushing beet red.

"Well, I hope you'll want to do that again."

I licked my lips and gave him a slight nod. "How far do you go with this? And how many before me?"

"I go as far as you feel comfortable. And there have been a few. But you're the first who's known anything about my club."

"So, none of your other...*partners*... have seen your room at the Sanctuary?"

"None of my other *partners* know I'm a Saint, Callie. They don't even know my name."

"How is that possible? They can enter your address into Google and find your property records."

"My brother and I have several companies. I bought it under one of those. It's hidden and it's hidden for a reason," he said.

"Well, then what do they call you?"

"Sir."

I couldn't stop a laugh. "Okay, I am not going to call

you Sir."

"You may enjoy it, baby."

"I don't think I'll be able to keep a straight face," I admitted.

He smiled. "Challenge accepted."

"Do you ever just have normal sex?"

"No. It's why our first night together was a mind fuck for me," he admitted, pulling me against him. "I wasn't prepared to enjoy it so much."

I smiled, sliding my hands up his chest. "Well, I have never, and I mean, *never*, taken a man home after a first date. Or whatever that was."

He kissed me gently. "It was a first date."

"Okay," I whispered.

He pulled a folded envelope from his back pocket and handed it to me. "I went to Eldie and had her run the full gamut of tests. These are the results. I'm clean. Are you up to date on your birth control?"

I nodded. "I have an IUD."

"You wanna play with me, Callie? Without condoms?"

I bit my lip. "Yes."

"You already wet?" he asked, sliding his hand up my skirt and between my legs.

"Yes."

His finger slid along the seam of my panties, then dipped inside of me. "Soaked."

I gripped his arm, bucking against his hand, but he pulled out of me and licked his finger clean. "Don't move."

He tugged my T-shirt over my head, unhooked my bra and dropped it onto the floor, then pushed my skirt and panties from my hips. I stepped out of the pile of fabric, leaving my flipflops under all of it, and he kicked the clothing into the corner of the room.

The coolness of his air-conditioned room made my nipples pebble and I couldn't stop a shiver, but I wasn't cold. I was needy.

He cupped my mound with a smile. "Spread your legs."

I did as he ordered, and he gave my pussy a gentle smack. "You just get waxed?"

I nodded.

"Sensitive?"

I nodded again, because I didn't think I could form words.

His fingers slid into me and his thumb grazed my clit, and I feared I'd come right there, but he must have known what he was doing and pulled away. I whimpered, reaching for his hand, but he shook his head. "You'll come when I tell you to come."

He walked to one of his cabinets, returning with a pair of nipple clamps that looked more like jewelry than a sex toy. Bending slightly, he sucked one nipple into a tighter peak, then settled the clamp over it, repeating the action with the other. A long chain with a crystal hung to my belly button and he tugged on it gently. "Too tight?"

I shook my head. God, it felt amazing.

He kissed me again. "I'll leave the pussy clamps for another time."

"Okay," I rasped, my body on overdrive as he moved his lips down my neck, his beard scraping deliciously across my skin.

He removed his clothes, slowly, torturously, and the second he freed his cock, I longed to taste it, but when I reached for him, he gave my ass a smack. "No."

"But—"

"Do I need to cuff you to the bed?"

"Maybe," I admitted. "I'm not the best at following

orders."

He grinned. "You want me to fuck you on your knees?"

"Oh, god, yes, please."

"Then, behave."

I sighed, rolling my shoulders in an effort to relax.

Sweet Pea chuckled. "Bend over the end of the bed. Grip the footboard and spread your legs. Wide, Callie. Don't make me tell you twice."

I stepped to the bed and did as he asked, although, I didn't quite spread as wide as I could, because I was hoping there'd be more spanking if I didn't.

He didn't disappoint and I moaned in pleasure when his hand connected with my bare flesh. There was a tiny hook at the end of the bed, and he hooked my chain to it, so that every time I moved, the clamps tugged on my nipples.

I heard the sound of a vibrator, then it was pressed against my opening and I desperately wanted to grind against it, but he had all the control.

"Pea," I begged.

He slipped it inside of me and I moaned as he moved it in and out of me, then slid it back to my ass. "You want me to play here again?"

"Yes," I panted out.

He pressed the vibrator against me, and I almost came undone. "You're gonna come, aren't you?"

I nodded, and he dropped the toy on the floor and unhooked me, guiding me onto the bed, burying himself inside of me from behind. I cried out as an orgasm washed over me, and then as he continued to thrust inside of me, another one built up and I was once again overwhelmed with pleasure as his cock practically hit my womb.

"Now!" I screamed, and he let out a grunt, his dick

pulsing as we fell in a heap on the bed, our bodies still connected, and breathing heavy as he wrapped his arms around me from behind and kissed the nape of my neck.

"So, you liked that," he observed.

"Oh my god," I panted out. "I have never experienced anything like that before. I want all of it."

"Well, pace yourself, baby. There's a lot of sex to be had, and I plan to explore every part of your body."

"I can get behind that," I said. "But first, do you have food? Because, I'm starving."

He grinned. "Yeah. Come on, we'll carb load, then I'll show you the wonders of anal."

"You know just what to say to a gal."

He laughed and led me back downstairs and into the kitchen.

* * *

The sound of rain hitting glass gently woke me and I reached for Sweet Pea only to find the bed empty. Sitting up, I wrapped the sheet around me and went to look for him.

"Pea?" I called out, walking downstairs.

He was pacing the living room, jeans slung low on his hips, shirtless and looking like the weight of the world was on his shoulders.

"There you are," I said. "Come to bed."

"No."

"Do you expect me to sleep alone?"

"Fuck!" he hissed. "We should go."

"It's three o'clock in the morning." He dragged his hands through his hair, and I closed the distance between us. "Hey, what's going on?"

"We can't sleep here. I don't sleep here."

I frowned. "I don't understand."

"Goddammit, Callie, you're turning my world upside down. I can't do this."

"Do what? Have sex then fall asleep?"

"I don't sleep here. This place is not for sleep. It's for sex. I'm not supposed to feel comfortable here. *You're* not supposed to feel comfortable here."

"You don't sleep here?" I asked, his words beginning to register. "Ever?"

He shook his head.

"So, you sleep at your girlfriends' place then?"

He shook his head.

"Honey, I really need you to start using words. Neanderthal wasn't my best subject in college, so I'm a little rusty on my grunts."

"I have never slept, as in, fallen asleep with a woman before."

I blinked up at him. "Seriously?"

"Seriously."

Somehow, this fact made my heart soar. "So, I popped your spooning cherry?"

His hand reached out and hooked around my neck, tugging me forward. "Why the fuck do you have to be funny *and* gorgeous?"

"Just cursed, I guess," I retorted.

He dropped his forehead to mine. "You make me feel safe, Callie, and that freaks me the fuck out."

"You are safe with me," I said, wrapping my arms around him. "I might not be able to fight off a gang of hardened criminals, but I'll protect your heart. Always."

He kissed me, tugging the sheet away from me and lifting me so I could wrap my legs around his waist, and then he carried me back to bed where we fell asleep in each other's arms.

* * *

"I'm gonna need you to keep those shoes on," Sweet

Pea informed me.

I grinned. I was wearing my favorite four-inch heeled, silver glitter Jimmy Choo sandals, and I had to admit, I knew they'd drive him wild. He'd just brought me home after dinner, and I had secretly hoped he'd take me back to his lair, but that didn't happen, so for now, I'd take what I could get.

"Oh yeah?"

He nodded. "Yeah."

I let us into my condo and he kicked the door closed behind us.

"What do you plan to do, big man?" I asked.

I found myself turned to face him and his large hand went to my throat. "You giving me a challenge, Callie?"

I pressed my lips into a thin line.

"Are you?"

I nodded and his mouth landed on mine. Hard.

When I reached for his cut, he grabbed my hands and pinned them behind my back. "No. Upstairs."

I rushed upstairs and into my bedroom, removing my clothing as I went, but keeping my shoes on, as he followed slowly. He walked into my closet, stepping out with one of my robe sashes.

"Leave your panties," he ordered, and I did, turning to face him. "You ready to play?"

I nodded.

Taking the sash, he tied my hands behind my back, leaning down to run his tongue across one nipple then the other. He stepped to my dresser and that was when I noticed he'd stopped in the kitchen for a bottle of bourbon and a glass of ice.

"I told you, I don't fuck around with ice in my whiskey," I said, but he ignored my comment.

Grabbing an ice cube, he peeled the front of my panties back and dropped the cube in, guiding it to my clit where he pressed it against my sensitive nub and secured it with the fabric. I shivered, whimpering as the cold did exactly what he intended.

"Callie?"

I swallowed, suddenly needing to squeeze my thighs together.

"Callie?"

"Hm?"

"Don't come."

I met his eyes. God, how did he know?

He squeezed my chin gently. "I'm gonna let you later, but you come now, we're done."

I bit my lip and nodded.

"If I use the riding crop, you gonna come?"

"Probably," I admitted.

"I'll wait, then."

"Thanks."

"You want ass play?"

"God, yes," I hissed. "But let's do that at the end too."

He chuckled. "My girl's a little wound up, huh?"

"You have no idea."

He kissed me, clamping my nipples while he did it, then removing his clothes, his huge dick already hard and ready. God, I wanted to wrap my mouth around him, but I knew he'd never allow it. I'd issued a challenge and that meant he was in charge.

He poured a shot of bourbon and helped me drink it, then took a shot himself before pouring another and setting it on the nightstand.

I'd ordered some extra toys to have at my place for the nights when we 'played' here, and I couldn't wait to see which ones he picked. I'd been very vocal about which ones were my favorites, so my anticipation was heightened when he stepped back into my closet. Grabbing my box of toys, he dropped it on the bed, pulling out a few with a grin before guiding me to stand against the wall. He turned my vibrator on and pressed it against my clit and I whimpered, the coldness and vibration nearly breaking me, but I forced myself not to come as he pressed a little harder.

When he pulled it away, I cried out, but he just smiled as he ripped my panties from my hips and slid the vibrator between my legs, turning it back on. He pressed it deep inside, my little rabbit hitting my clit as he maneuvered it to just the right spot. I arched, unable to do anything else with my hands tied behind my back.

"Do you know how fuckin' beautiful you are?" he rasped.

Before I could respond, the vibrator was dropped on the floor, my hands were untied, and his dick was inside of me as he was pounding into me, my back against the wall. I wrapped my legs around him, slid my hands into his hair, and pressed my clamped nipples to his chest.

It hurt.

In the best of ways.

Sweet Pea slid his finger into my mouth and said, "Suck."

I did, and he removed it before pressing it into my very private place.

"Oh, god, yes," I hissed.

It wasn't long before I knew I was going to lose all control. So much for my challenge.

"Now, baby."

He carried me to the bed and lay me flat while he stood at the edge of the mattress and pulled out.

"What the fuck?" I growled.

"I told you I'd let you come, but it'd be on my time."

He took the shot glass off the nightstand and dribbled a little bourbon on my mound, quickly licking it off me and I arched against his mouth.

"Pea, please," I begged.

"You concedin'?"

"If it means you're going to let me come, yes."

He grinned, hovering over me. "You sure?"

"I'm sure."

He kissed me, burying himself deep again, before slamming into me harder and harder until I screamed his name, my pussy contracting around his pulsing cock as we fell in a heap on the sheets.

I was still wearing my heels and nipple clamps.

Sweet Pea grinned, kissing me quickly before removing both and then pulling me over his chest.

"I knew I'd get you to say my name," he said, with a smirk.

"Well, aren't you the cocky one?"

"Not at all," Sweet Pea replied, seemingly unphased by my dig at him.

"No?"

"Cockiness is a disguise worn to mask insecurities. I'm confident. There's a big difference between confident and cocky."

"Legally speaking, of course," I teased.

"I'm not sure my definition would hold up in court but let me put it this way. Confidence is being fully relaxed when your old lady is out on the town with her girlfriends."

"Because you know she's not going to cheat on you?" I replied rhetorically.

"No. Because when women are together for long enough, they eventually start talking shit about their men, right?"

"I suppose."

"C'mon counselor, you should know better than to lie under oath," he teased and gently tickled my ribs.

I squirmed and he held me tighter. "Okay," I admitted with a giggle. "So, you're confident that when your 'old lady' is out with her friends that she won't talk shit about you."

"No, that's not it at all. I fully expect her to talk shit about me."

"What?"

"Sure. I'm sure I would have earned every lash of the whip."

"Then what are you so confident about?"

"Because I'd know that whatever grievances she had against me weren't related to the bedroom. No matter what she may say to her girlfriends, it would never be that I didn't make her come 'til she couldn't see straight."

"Oh my god, you're insane."

"But I'm right."

I straddled his hips, leaning down to kiss him. "I'm not sure. I think you need to show me something more."

He grinned, flipping me onto my back and showing me a hell of a lot more than I was expecting.

* * *

"Can I ask you a personal question?" I asked as we finished dressing.

"Shoot."

"Not that I'm complaining or anything, but have you noticed every time we start to get personal, we have sex? I feel as though we're not really getting to know each other on a soul level if all we do is fuck."

"What's wrong with fucking?" Sweet Pea challenged.

"Nothing. I love it. But I want to know you. Know what makes you tick."

"Read the file," he said, coldly.

"Come on, don't be like that."

"Be like what?"

"Cagey about your past. I'm trying to understand you better, but I can't do that if I don't know anything about you."

"Let me ask you something," he said. "When you look back on your childhood, do you have mostly good memories?"

"Yes, of course."

"See? You say of course, like a happy childhood is typical."

"You don't think that's true?" I asked.

"Not from my experience. Most of the Saints grew up in shitty homes with parents who were in and out of jail themselves."

"But you didn't," I said.

"No, but just because I grew up rich, doesn't mean my home life was good."

"I didn't say anything about money, I was talking about your parents. You had a mom and a dad and a seemingly stable life. What made you decide to run away?"

"Why is it so important to you to know why?"

"I have to confess something to you," I said, feeling a pang of guilt in the pit of my stomach.

"What is it?"

"That first night, at Sally Anne's I told you my mother was killed in a car accident."

"I remember."

"That's not actually true. My mother wasn't killed, she abandoned me and my father. One day, without warning, she decided she didn't want to be a wife and mother and left without a word. I was thirteen years old."

"So, your mother is alive?"

"No, she died from a heroin overdose four years after she left."

"Jesus, Callie," Sweet Pea said softly.

"My father later told me she'd become addicted to opioids shortly before she left us, and that he'd been too consumed with his work to notice until it was too late."

"That shit gets a grip on some people," he said.

"I'm still working through the guilt I feel for not noticing my mother's problems myself."

"You were just a kid," Sweet Pea said.

"I know that now, and it's because of what I went through that I decided to practice family law. To do what I could to help keep families together."

"Why lie to me about your mother? You didn't do anything wrong."

"Because despite my progress, it's still painful for me to talk about, but mostly because I don't want people looking at me the way you're looking at me right now."

"Then why tell me?"

"Because I have a fear of abandonment, and knowing you ran from what appears to be a stable home, scares me."

"Why?" he asked dryly.

"Well, I guess I figured since you invited me to Clutch and Eldie's party, and after last night, that you were interested in pursuing some sort of a relationship with me."

Sweet Pea looked at the floor and said nothing. This was clearly not the conversation he was expecting or wanting to have.

"Did I say something wrong?"

"No," he said. "I...I don't really have the time to talk about all of this right now. I've got a bunch of shit I need to get done at the Sanctuary today. I should really get going."

With that, Sweet Pea gave me a kiss on the forehead and left me by myself in the condo.

TWELVE

BURNING SAINTS

Sweet Pea

"**B**ECAUSE THAT'S NOT how I fucking told you to do it, that's why," I snapped.

"My way will take half the time," Doozer argued.

"No, it's gonna take you twice as long, because now you have to remove this piece of shit wiring harness and replace it with the right one," I said.

"That's gonna mean a trip to Big Ernie's to find another one that'll work on a '68."

"Then you'd better leave now."

I'd been in a shitty mood all day, and Doozer was not helping matters in any way. Elwood was sick, so I was filling in at the club's shop and we were behind schedule on a vintage Triumph restoration job. I volunteered for the job because I thought it would help take my mind off Callie, but in truth, just the opposite was happening. I was irritable, distracted, and having a hard time focusing.

"Traffic's gonna be hell. I'll send a recruit," he said.

"No. It's your mistake and you're gonna fix it, so get on your bike and fucking ride," I growled.

Doozer threw down his plyers and walked away without another word.

I returned to finishing my work on the bike's gas tank and tried, unsuccessfully, not to think of Callie. Why did everything have to be so damned complicated? Why the hell did I have to meet her now, at the worst possible time?

Minus approached just as I was finishing my last weld.

"Any word from the Spiders?" I asked after raising the visor on my helmet.

"Why is that the first question everyone asks as soon as they see me?"

"I guess we're on pins and needles," I replied.

"Where's Doozer?"

"He had to run to Big Ernie's for a wiring harness for that '68," I said motioning to the Triumph.

"Who'd he take with him?" Minus asked.

"Dunno. Spike is on the gate and Tacky is working out."

"He probably took Trouble."

"He'd better start focusing on his fuckin' job and less on pussy," I said.

"Everything going okay with those two?" he asked, obviously noting the irritation in my voice.

I removed my helmet and tossed it on the workbench. "They're good, I'm just in a pissy mood."

"Why don't you take a page from the young lovers' book and go see your woman tonight?"

"Callie isn't my woman."

"You sure about that?" Minus asked. "Seems to me like she makes you happy."

"What the fuck is wrong with everyone around here? Yeah, Callie's great. So what?"

"If she's great, what's the problem?"

"Timing, for one thing."

Minus smiled wide and placed a hand on my shoulder. "There's never a good time to fall in love."

"Fuck that noise," I said.

"I was watching the two of you at the party and I know what I saw."

"I don't give a shit what you think you saw, or how good Callie makes me feel. The whole situation has been messy from the start and it's only gonna get messier if I keep seeing her."

"So, that's it then?"

"I'd have thought you would have been happy for me to get rid of such a big distraction."

"Yeah, you seem so much more focused and relaxed right now."

"Minus, trying to figure out how to fit Callie into my life is making me crazy. We still don't know if the Spiders are gonna move on us, I now have four soldiers that I'm responsible for, and I'm still trying to figure out my long-term earning plan for the club. It'd be better for both Callie and me if I call it before shit gets out of hand."

"You've gotta do what you think is best, but let me say two things first and then I'll drop it. Cool?"

I nodded. Minus was as straight a shooter as they came and, next to my brother, was the man I respected the most. So as much as I didn't want to, I listened.

"You've been a great soldier and I have no doubt you'll prove to be a great officer. Your loyalty to the club is without question and you never hesitate to put the needs of your brothers before your own."

"Thanks."

"It's not so much praise as it is stating the truth, but I worry about you."

"Me?"

"It seems to me like you have a shot at being happy and I'm worried you'll let it pass you by out of misguided loyalty to the club."

"Misguided?"

"This club can't be the only love in your life, Pea."

"I owe the club everything," I said.

"The books seem pretty fuckin' balanced from where I stand."

"I'd be dead if it wasn't for the Saints."

"You'll die inside if you don't start thinking about yourself for once."

Minus was right. I clearly had some personal shit to work on, but I still didn't see how dragging Callie into any of it would be good for her.

* * *

Callie

I hadn't heard from Sweet Pea for almost two days and I was beginning to freak out. Was he ghosting me? We'd had three weeks of mind-blowing sex and change the world kind of conversations, so I thought we were solidifying something beautiful here.

My phone buzzed and Sweet Pea's name popped up on the screen. I answered immediately. "Hi. Are you okay?"

"Yeah. Just been a shitty past few days."

"Well, I can make it better. Just say the word," I offered.

"Yeah, ah, I think we should talk."

"Fuck," I breathed out. "Why?"

"Just really think it would be a good idea."

"If you're dumping me, do it over the phone like a normal human," I snapped. "Don't do it somewhere I'll be mortified."

"Callie, I'm sorry. This just isn't working."

"Next you'll say, 'It isn't you, it's me,'" I said sadly.

"I wouldn't insult your intelligence, even if it's true."

"Fine, whatever, *Charles*. Have a nice fucking life."

I hung up, closed and locked my office door, and dissolved in a puddle of tears on my office sofa. I gave myself exactly twenty-five minutes to be sad, and then I stood up, opened my makeup drawer, and reapplied my 'face.'

Fuck Sweet Pea and the bike he rode in on.

* * *

Sweet Pea

I knew it was for the best that I hit the brakes on this thing with Callie, but I still felt like shit about our conversation. I told myself, over and over that she was an amazing woman and deserved a life with a man who was better than me, but the mere thought of her with someone else twisted my guts in a knot. Despite what Minus, Clutch, and even my brother had to say, I had to walk away before either of us got in any deeper, even though it was the last thing I wanted to do.

Since I couldn't work on the Triumph until Doozer got back, I closed the shop and went for a ride to cool off and clear my head.

I arrived back at the Sanctuary at sunset. Massive clouds painted with vibrant streaks of pink and orange filled the winter skies as the sun said its final goodbye for the day. Kitty was stationed at the guard tower and opened the gate as soon as I pulled up. I parked my bike and made my way inside.

I walked into the Sanctuary to find it empty. Socks was on guard duty in the great hall and appeared to be the only one around.

"Hey, Socks. Where is everyone?"

"Minus is in his office," he replied. "Clutch and most of the guys are watching the UFC fight down in the basement, a couple of others rode out a few hours ago. Your brother's somewhere, probably fuckin' Devlin."

"What the fuck about me makes you think I'd want to think of my brother's sex life?"

Socks shrugged.

"No issues tonight?" I asked.

"Not so far."

The streets had been eerily quiet since our show of force with the Spiders. I didn't know if Wolf would back down, but at the very least he knew the Saints and our allies weren't fucking around. We were prepared to protect our clubs and our territories, so if Wolf was smart, his answer would be peace.

"I'm gonna go watch the fight."

I headed to the kitchen first to grab a beer and heard the roar of pipes, followed by a gunshot and then another. The sounds were coming from just outside the compound gate.

I set the beer down and ran out in time to see Kitty shooting his rifle at a fleeing rider.

"Who the fuck was that?" I shouted.

"I dunno," Kitty replied. "The mother fucker rode up, threw something down in the street and fired a shot before speeding off."

"He took a shot at you?"

"No, in the air, but I wasn't taking any fuckin' chances. Ya know?"

Minus, Clutch, and Ropes came running followed by the rest of the club.

"Some sort of half-assed drive by or something," Kitty yelled down to Minus.

"Could you see a patch?"

"Spiders. Looked like a prospect patch." Kitty replied.

"What the hell is that in the street?" Clutch asked, motioning to whatever the rider had dropped.

"I don't know, but we're not getting close enough to find out. Could be a bomb for all we know."

"Fuck that," Clutch said, and made a bee line for the mystery package.

"Clutch!" Minus yelled, but his best friend and Sergeant at Arms paid him no mind.

Clutch returned with what looked like a pillow made of plastic wrap, and we gave him a wide berth as he walked by.

"Pussies," Clutch said as he walked past us and into the Sanctuary.

We followed Clutch inside and he placed the package on the kitchen counter. He pulled out his blade and carefully began to cut away at the outer layers of the curious packaging.

"Please don't blow us all up, for fuck's sake," Minus said as Clutch continued his delicate surgery. We looked on in total silence as Clutch continued, curious to see what the fuck this was all about. We wouldn't have to wait long.

Inside the tightly wrapped plastic cocoon was a Burning Saints kutte, completely covered in blood.

"Motherfuckers," Clutch seethed.

He took his thumb and wiped the blood away to reveal a patch that read DOOZER.

"I'll kill them all," Clutch said.

"We don't know that he's actually dead, right?" Socks asked, his voice breaking up slightly. "I mean, the Spiders could just be fucking with us, right?"

Clutch opened Doozer's kutte wide to reveal a human heart placed within it.

We finally had Wolf's answer and it was war.

* * *

My field of vision narrowed, and my heart pounded so hard I thought I was gonna pass out. I steadied myself on the counter as my brain tried to make sense of what was laid out in front of us.

"I swear to God, I'll kill every one of those evil motherfuckers," Clutch yelled.

"The only thing you're gonna do right now is keep your shit together," Minus said. "You got me, Sergeant?"

"They killed Doozer, Minus. They cut his fucking heart out," Clutch snapped.

"You think I can't see that?" Minus asked. "Doozer's death doesn't change anything. We have to be smart."

"Doesn't change anything? How the fuck can you say that?" I challenged Minus, my rage reaching its boiling point.

"That's enough, Pea," Ropes admonished.

"Fuck that," I snapped. "The Spiders killing Doozer changes everything. This is a declaration of war, plain and simple. Not to mention, who Wolf chose to take out.

Doozer was my guy and Wolf fucking knew it. He did this to punish me, Minus. Doozer was my guy!"

"And this is my club," Minus growled. "I'll say the same thing to you as I said to Clutch. Sit down and don't move a fucking muscle without my say so. This isn't church and I'm not asking for everyone's votes. I'm telling every Saint within the sound of my voice to stay cool and wait for further instructions before doing anything. Do you all understand me?"

Before anyone could respond, our attention was drawn to Trouble, who had frantically pushed her way through the crowd of Saints now gathered in the kitchen.

"Is it true?" Trouble screamed as she made her way to the counter.

"Trouble, don't," I said, trying unsuccessfully to shield her from the scene.

"No! Doozer!" Trouble cried out at the horror on display.

I pulled her near to comfort her but a sharp elbow to my ribs caused me to let her go.

Trouble stood trembling, her eyes locked on Doozer's kutte. "Tell me where the Spiders' club house is," she said in an unsteady voice, to no one in particular.

"Going there would be a bad idea," Minus replied calmly.

Trouble looked up at Minus, then to me before asking, this time very clearly, "Where are the Spiders?"

"They're gonna pay," I tried to reassure her.

"The only way they pay, is if we make them pay!" she yelled before bolting for the exit.

"Trouble, wait!" I called after her, but she had already managed to snake her way through the crowd and out the door.

"Goddammit," I huffed.

I didn't know Trouble well enough to know how she'd handle Doozer's death. Hell, I didn't know how I was gonna deal with it. I knew for sure I wanted blood, and clearly Trouble wanted the same. The question was, how far would she be willing to go to get it?

"Don't worry," Minus said to me. "We're on full lock down. That means nobody in or out. They'll stop her at the gate if she tries to do anything impulsive."

I nodded, but his assurance didn't make me feel much better. So far, one of the soldiers under my command was dead and another was unhinged.

"Officers, in the Chapel now," Minus said. "Everyone else, find something useful to do."

I spotted Spike and Tacky and waved them over to me.

"Find Trouble. Make sure she's okay and report back to me as soon as you have eyes on her." They nodded and took off, and I made my way to the Chapel with Minus and the other officers.

Minus began as soon as the door was closed, "Clutch, I want Eldie here to preserve Doozer's…remains."

"We're not cops working a crime scene, Minus," Clutch replied.

"Jesus Christ," Minus bellowed. "Can anyone in this fucking club follow an order?"

The room fell silent at Minus's uncharacteristic outburst.

"Listen to me very closely, every one of you," he continued. "You're not the only ones tore up over Doozer. I want to hit the Spiders back just as badly as you do, but that's exactly what they're expecting. We need to keep our cool and plan our next move carefully or we'll play right into their hands."

"What do you need?" Clutch asked, calmly.

"We need intel, which is why I want the doc here. If there's any data to be collected from Doozer's kutte and heart I want to make sure it's as preserved and uncontaminated as possible, okay?"

"I'll ride out with Hacksaw in one of the work vans and pick her up from the clinic," he said.

"Thank you," Minus said, before addressing the room once again, "This is war, gentlemen. Doozer is our first casualty and we need to do everything within our power to make sure he's the last."

"Does that include fire power?" Clutch asked.

"We've worked so hard to become the club Cutter envisioned," Minus said, his voice filled with sorrow, before whispering, "God damn you, Wolf," and nodding to Clutch.

"Listen up," Clutch said, addressing the room as if he'd rehearsed this moment. "Every Saint is to carry a pistol at all times, and no one rides without body armor. For those of you that don't already have a pistol stashed away, or are comfortable with carrying something a little heavier, talk to me or Kitty."

"The rules still apply, gentlemen. These weapons are to be used for self-defense only. No retaliation and no first blood. Do you understand?"

The room responded in nods and grunts.

My phone buzzed. It was a message from Spike.

Trouble got out. She left her bike and hopped the fence.

"Shit," I said, jumping to my feet.

"What is it?" Minus asked.

"Trouble, she's gone. I have to find her."

"Hold on," he said.

"Goddammit, Minus. She's out there and she's gonna get herself killed. I'm not gonna lose another Saint tonight. I fucking can't."

Minus nodded and I was out the door.

"Take someone with you," I heard Minus through the closed door, but paid no mind. I worked better alone and didn't need anyone slowing me down. Trouble couldn't have gotten too far without her bike so this shouldn't take long anyway.

I rolled through the Sanctuary gates and off into the night in search of our lost lamb. The sound of my bike my only comfort as I rode.

I'd combed the Sanctuary's surrounding area for five minutes and saw no sign of Trouble. Tracking a street-smart kid like her was going to be next to impossible, but I had to try.

Come on baby girl, where are you?

I had no idea what Trouble had with her when she left the Sanctuary. Did she take a laptop? Did she have a gun? My heart knotted up at the thought of what the Spiders would do to her if they caught her, or what *I* would do to them if they laid a finger on her. The whole situation was made worse by the fact that as stupid as Trouble was for running off half-cocked like this, I related to her one hundred percent. I knew exactly how helpless and angry she felt, and I wanted nothing more than to tear Wolf's throat out for killing Doozer. In fact, I wasn't at all sure that I wouldn't try the moment I saw him. All I knew was, I couldn't let Trouble become the next victim of the Spiders' endless cycle of violence and death.

What if she found out the location of the Spiders' Clubhouse and managed to hotwire a car?

I spun my bike around and headed toward the freeway. If Trouble was on her way to Gresham, I still had a chance to head her off at the pass. I flew down Forrester, crossing over Pine when I was nearly deafened by the sound of metal impacting metal and blinded by an intense white light.

THIRTEEN

BURNING SAINTS

Taxi

"**W**AS MY MESSAGE sent?" Wolf sneered.

"Loud and clear," I said, setting the digital camera on Wolf's desk. He scrolled through the photos and smiled wide.

"Doozer give you any trouble?"

"Just enough to make the job fun," I replied.

"And the package?"

"FedEx couldn't have delivered it better."

"You were right, Trunk," Wolf said turning to his V.P., pointing at me. "This man does have ice water in his veins."

"Any word from Sweet Pea?" Wolf asked Trunk.

"The minute Flash has eyes...or *eye* on him, he'll let us know," he replied.

"I want Sweet Pea."

"Yes, Boss."

Wolf reached into the bottom drawer of his desk and produced a bottle and a Spiders' patch. "Sounds like it's time to toast our newest Spider." He poured out shots for the three of us and we raised our glasses. "To Taxi. Who I think, after seeing those photos, should really consider a new career as a butcher."

"Jesus, that's some welcome speech. You trying to get rid of me already?"

Wolf smiled before knocking his shot back. "No, sir. In fact, I think you're gonna turn out to be quite useful."

"Hold on a second," Trunk said, placing his hand over his kutte pocket. "It's the burner," he said, producing a cell phone and answering.

"Hello? Just now? Okay, meet us at the location. We're on our way," he said before hanging up while grinning ear to ear. "Get ready to be really fucking happy, Boss."

* * *

The garage bay door slammed shut as soon as the truck pulled inside. Flash stepped out grinning ear to ear.

"You shoulda seen that big motherfucker fly!" he shouted gleefully.

"Shut the fuck up," Wolf growled. "Is he dead?"

"I didn't exactly stick around to find out, but if Sweet Pea is still alive, he's gonna be riding the 'short bike' from now on if you know what I mean," Flash said, laughing at his own joke.

"I hit him at just the right spot, Wolf. No witnesses. Just like you planned. It was fucking beautiful."

"You'd better have taken him out permanently or I'm gonna take the one good eye you've got left. Now, chop up the truck and get it the fuck outta here before anything can be traced back to us."

Flash stopped smiling and began his task of making a five-thousand-pound truck disappear.

"There's no way Minus can ignore me now," Wolf said. "He'll have to come after me, and when he does, he'll find out what else I have in store for him and the 'Burning Taints.'"

"I'd be more worried about Ropes than Minus," Trunk said. "When he hears about you taking Sweet Pea out, he's going to come at you with those famous plyers of his."

"Let him fucking try and I'll make it a lot harder for him to type," Wolf said.

"What about the other clubs?" Trunk asked.

"If the Dogs of Fire and Primal Howlers want to stand with the Saints, then they can fall with them too. Now that Char isn't around to stop me, I'm going to unleash hell on all those motherfuckers. I have business to do and these candy-ass pretend bikers keep getting in my way."

"You sure you're not underestimating your old club just a little?" Trunk asked. "I know Minus is on some sort of self-improvement, time's up, vision quest, or whatever, but from the way you tell it, the Saints are no strangers to getting wet."

"I know exactly what lines Minus and the Burning Saints will and won't cross. Same goes for the other clubs. They all abide by some sort of goodie-goodie bullshit code of conduct. They all live under self-imposed rules about who you can and cannot kidnap, rape, torture and kill."

I'd heard more than my fair share of hard talk by

hard men, but Wolf's words made my blood run cold.

"I'll tell you the same thing I told Char before his unfortunate accident. I will stop at nothing to make the Spiders the largest, most feared, and most profitable motorcycle club in the country. Nothing."

"What about the cops?" I knew I was taking a big risk by opening my mouth, especially given Wolf's excited state, but it was a calculated move on my part. I knew, with a guy like Wolf, that if I didn't start including myself in his plans, I could risk being left out of them.

Wolf spun around to face me. "It's only because you're new that I'm gonna give you a pass for interrupting me. Once."

"I'm all for your scorched earth plan," I continued without flinching, "but what about the police?"

"What the fuck about them?"

"From the results of tonight's activities, it occurs to me that bodies of dead bikers are gonna start piling up in the streets of Portland. That tends to get the attention of law enforcement."

"You let me fucking worry about the law. I've got that handled," Wolf snapped. "Yet one more Ace we're holding that the Saints don't have."

"And Los Psychos?" Trunk squeaked out.

"What the fuck is this? Question and answer time with Uncle Wolfie? What the fuck do you wanna know about the Mexicans?"

"It's just that you mentioned the Dogs of Fire and the Primal Howlers, who may not pose much of a threat, but what about Los Psychos? Those guys are as hardcore as it gets, and they outnumber us."

"South of the border, but not here," Wolf corrected. "Besides, El Cacto is an old man with a bad heart."

"He's still an O.G."

"With O.G. views, which makes him predictable and weak. Of course, he sided with the Burning Saints. They're in business together, and El Cacto still thinks loyalty pays the bills. He also thinks all those gym rat pretty boys are going to be able to protect his frail ass when the shit goes down. He's dead wrong on both counts, and soon enough he'll know that."

Wolf threw his hands in the air and looked around.

"Now, if there are no more fucking questions, how 'bout you assholes chop up this truck."

* * *

Minus

Sweet Pea bolted out the door with clearly no intention of listening to me about riding with a wingman.

I turned to his brother, Ropes. "What the fuck makes him so pigheaded?"

"Genesis, chapter four, verse nine," Ropes replied. "Then the Lord said to Cain, 'Where is Abel your brother?' He said, 'I do not know, am I my brother's keeper?'"

"So, in this scenario, I'm God, and you've killed Sweet Pea?"

"There are days when I'd like to," Ropes replied in a way only a brother could.

I leaned over to Warthog and asked, "Go find Spike and Tacky and tell 'em to catch up with Sweet Pea, will ya?"

"10-4," Warthog rasped, and ducked out of the room before returning a minute later, giving me a thumbs up.

I brought the meeting back to order and got down to business. Now that I knew Wolf was intent on expanding the Spiders' territory into Portland, we knew what our next steps would be. I reminded each officer of their orders and reviewed the current inventory of our armory and the Sanctuary pantry. In the event of a lock down, I wanted every Saint and their families to be able to hunker down here safely and comfortably for as long as needed.

We'd covered everything I needed to, and I was ready to adjourn when Tacky came bursting through the door, covered in sweat.

"It's... Sweet Pea. He's... been hit," he said, panting heavily.

"Where is he?" I asked.

"He's on Forrester. Spike's with him. He called 9-1-1."

"Hit? Was he shot?" Ropes asked, frantically.

"No, someone ran him down in the intersection."

Ropes was out the door before I could say another word.

"Me and Spike had almost caught up to Sweet Pea," Tacky continued. "We had just ridden past Larch Street and could see him just one block ahead of us. He was crossing the intersection and a black truck came barreling through without slowing down at all. They smashed right into him and didn't stop for a second."

"Sweet Pea is alive though?"

"He was when I left him with Spike, but he was pretty fucked up, Minus," Tacky said softly. "They rammed him at full-speed."

"Did you get a good look at the truck?"

"I'm sorry Minus. All I know for sure is that it was black. As in, all black. You know, like murdered out and shit."

"Alright, good job, Tacky," I said and pulled out my phone to call Spike.

He picked up right away and I could hear sirens in the background.

"He's alive but he's in bad shape, Minus."

"I'm on my way," I said and hung up.

* * *

"You look terrible." Cricket's voice stirred me awake from my uneasy slumber on my makeshift waiting room bed.

"Thanks, Sweetness. You know just what to say to a guy."

Cricket bent down and kissed me.

"What time is it?" I asked.

"It's four A.M. You told me to wake you in an hour. Do you want to go back to sleep?"

"No, I'm glad you woke me," I said, sitting up. "How's Pea?"

"Still in surgery." I dragged my hands down my face. "It's a miracle he's alive, Cricket."

Sweet Pea had a brain bleed, which could have been much worse had he not been wearing a helmet, but it was enough of a concern that they'd put him in a medically induced coma for a few days. Two broken ribs, aortic aneurysm, collapsed right lung, deep right thigh puncture, broken left femur, broken tibia and fibula, broken left and right ankles and his pelvis was broken in three places.

"Spiders?" she asked.

"It had to be. The timing and location were just too perfect for it to be a random accident."

"No sign of the truck that hit him?"

"That area of town is poorly lit and there are no surveillance or traffic cameras anywhere. It's all residential and there are rarely pedestrians out at this time of night. Besides, if it was the Spiders, that truck is long gone by now."

"You think they were stalking him?"

"Sweet Pea told me Wolf killing Doozer was some sort of message. That Wolf meant it as a personal attack on him."

"And you think he's right?"

"I didn't at the time. I figured he was feeling guilty about Doozer, but what if he was?"

"It makes sense," Cricket said. "Sweet Pea was Wolf's protégé and now Doozer is his. Sweet Pea not only rejected, but humiliated Wolf when he asked him to go with him to the Spiders."

"I always knew Wolf was a sonofabitch, but this..."

"*This* is exactly the kind of thing you've been trying to avoid. It's why you've been working so hard to build a new future for the club," Cricket said.

"Yeah, but now it's bleeding into friendlies."

"Like?"

"Doc said they've been messing with them in Savannah."

Doc was the chapter president of the Dogs of Fire MC in Savannah, and the Spiders had already bombed the VP's home. Doc and I had been friends for years, long before I'd patched into the Saints, and I felt responsible that my shit was bleeding onto his.

I sighed. "What we view as positive change, our enemies see as weakness. A reason to come after us."

Cricket stroked my cheek. "You knew they would."

"True, but now we have one Saint in the ICU and another inside a cooler in Eldie's fridge."

"And that changes how you should run the club?"

"Of course it does. My number one job is to keep every club member safe."

"Is it?" Cricket challenged. "I'm not sure your brothers would agree with you about that. They're grown-ass men that can protect themselves. You're the President of an MC, not a fucking den mother."

Cricket was adorable when she got fired up, and truth be told, her motivational speech was helping.

"You're the best co-captain I could ask for," I said leaning in for a kiss.

"Cutter knew what he was doing," she said smiling.

"I think he'd be rip fuckin' roaring pissed if he knew the club was riding heavy again ."

"The Spiders have guns, right?"

I nodded.

"Then you'd be foolish to be out there carrying snowballs," she pointed out.

"Maybe," I said. "But I can't help feeling like this is a giant step backwards for the Saints."

"You didn't ask for this war."

"No, but I could make it a hell of a lot worse. Putting more guns on the street could mean more people die. Innocent people."

"That's why you're the President. To make sure things like that don't happen. To be the example of strength and restraint," she said.

"Then there's Sweet Pea. I think I'm gonna call Doc and see if he can fly out and help Eldie with the rehab set up. He's more experienced in this area, having helped wounded soldiers in the past."

"I think that's an excellent idea," Cricket said. "He'll be good to have here for backup as well, because I'll tell you one thing for sure. If Sweet Pea dies, nothing will be able to restrain Ropes."

I held her for a few precious minutes, knowing she'd never spoken a more frightening truth.

* * *

Taxi

"You're gonna miss your target by two meters," I said,

and pressed the muzzle of my gun into the back of the hooded would-be assassin, who froze instantly. "Now, slowly take your hands off the weapon and place both hands behind your back, with your palms facing away from each other. Do you understand?"

The sniper nodded and followed my instructions.

"I'm gonna cuff you and sit you up, and if you give me a hard time, I'll give you a harder one," I said.

I sat the sniper up and was shocked to see the face of a pretty young girl underneath the black hooded sweat-shirt.

"And, who might you be?" I asked but got nothing but a sneer in return. "Well, you're sure as hell not a D.M., that's for sure, but that's a nice Ruger you've got there."

"Don't touch my gun," she said.

"Not really in much of a position to give me orders, are you?"

"Fuck you."

"Plus," I continued, "that's a rifle, not a gun. If you knew the difference, maybe you would have had a chance at hitting your target."

"I wouldn't have missed," she hissed.

"Yes, you would have. By at least two meters. Partially because your scope is set up incorrectly, but mainly because you weren't compensating for spin drift."

"So, maybe I would have missed the first shot, but I could have gotten off at least one more before he took cover."

"Not before I blew your brains out," I replied.

"So why haven't you?"

"Tango would have. You're lucky I'm the one guarding the west side of the ridge tonight and not him."

"If you're planning on trying to rape me, you should just kill me now, because I will fuck you up even with my hands behind my back."

"Relax, I'm not going to hurt you."

"What are you going to do with me?"

"That depends on who you are and why you're trying to kill Wolf."

"I'm Trouble."

"I'll bet you are," I said.

"It's my name, dickhead."

"Trouble, huh? Sounds like a club name. Is Wolf the estranged father who walked out on you?"

Trouble made unbroken eye contact with me for the first time.

"You don't know the first thing about my father. Wolf isn't worthy to lick dog shit from the bottom of my father's boots."

"That leaves business," I said. "Am I gonna find a kutte underneath that hoodie?"

"I'd advise against looking," she said, and I didn't doubt her.

"This is about Doozer isn't it?" I asked.

Trouble stiffened.

"You were his woman, weren't you?" I asked, unable to fight back a smile.

"What the fuck is so funny?" Trouble seethed.

"You need to come with me, right now," I said.

FOURTEEN

Sweet Pea

I WAS NO stranger to pain. My childhood was filled with it. Despite my cool exterior, pain burned inside me as fuel. It wasn't the cleanest energy source, but it got the job done and was in abundant supply.

I'd laid awake in darkness for the third night in a row, the medication dispenser button gripped tight in my sweaty hand, as I counted down the seconds until I'd be able to self-administer the next dose. As great as the pain was throughout my body, it couldn't rival the sorrow I felt in my heart. I prayed the meds would help dull both.

The timer on the medication pump beeped only once

before my thumb pressed down on the button, providing the much-needed cocktail to course through my broken body. My physical pain subsided greatly, and my eyelids became heavy. As I drifted into twilight, I became more and more aware of the hum of the machinery surrounding my bed. My body began to feel weightless as if it wanted to rise out of my bed, while dark thoughts kept my mind anchored to the earth.

* * *

Callie

Two weeks, three days, and four hours. That's how long it had been since Sweet Pea dumped me on my ass and how long I'd felt like my heart was disintegrating.

God! This was so stupid. I wasn't some high school girl whose boyfriend had been caught behind the bleachers with a cheerleader. But, why did I feel like that?

Because he was the best lay you've ever had.

It was more than that, though.

The big dumb Viking had gotten under my skin, and I was pretty sure I'd gotten under his, too. But he was freaked, and I didn't exactly understand how deep that fear went.

The ringing of my office phone dragged me out of my maudlin thoughts, and I picked it up. "Callie Ames."

"Hey, Callie, it's Cowboy."

"Hey, Cowboy, how are you?"

"I'm just reachin' out to see if you need anything."

Cowboy and I had only one brief email exchange since our introduction, so I was a bit surprised and confused by his call.

"I'm good as far as I know," I replied.

"Glad to hear you're holding up," he said. "And

how's the patient?"

Now I was really confused. "The patient?"

"Sweet Pea. How's he recovering from the crash?"

My heart raced. "Um...I'm sorry?"

"The crash," he said, followed by a long pause. "Aw, fuck, sweetheart, you didn't know?"

I stood, biting back tears. "Ah, sorry, Cowboy, can I call you back?"

I didn't wait for him to respond as I hung up my phone and rummaged through my purse for my cell, but I realized quickly I didn't know who the hell to call. Wiping tears away with the back of my hand, I opened my laptop and pulled up Bing.

Shit, what was the name of that fucking clinic?

Neighborhood something?

Shit, shit, shit!

It took me a moment of searching, but then Good Neighbor Medical Clinic popped up, along with a lovely photo of Dr. Gina Gardner, which was the only doctor mentioned, so I pulled out my phone and dialed the number.

"Good Neighbor Medical, how may I help you?"

"I was wondering if Dr. Gardner was available, please?"

"She's with a patient, may I ask who's calling?"

"Ah, my name is Callie Ames. I don't think she'll know who I am, but would you have her call me back, please?"

"And what's it regarding?"

I squeezed my eyes closed. "Sweet Pea."

"Okay, Ms. Ames, I'll give her the message."

"Thank you," I said, and hung up.

Unable to focus on anything else, I packed up my laptop and told my assistant I was leaving for the day, before heading down to Gregg's office. Knocking on his door, I entered when bid and sat in the chair in front of his desk. "I need to take a couple of personal days."

"Why?"

"It's personal," I said.

He sighed, dropping the pen he'd been holding on the desk. "Callie, you're barely here as it is."

"Well, I don't think that's fair."

"Isn't it?"

"No. Look, Gregg, I was promised that my position here would be one that would make a difference. I told you I wanted to help kids and families heal from trauma, and so far, all I've managed to do is help you win a few cases and further your career. But mostly I'm treated like a glorified consultant, whose advice isn't taken most of the time, by the way."

"Now, don't get testy," he grumbled.

"Jesus Christ, Gregg, if you want testy, I'll show you fucking testy."

"I don't think that language is called for, Callie."

"Well, how about this language?" I said, standing. "Please, sir, take your job and shove it up your ass. Consider this my two-weeks' notice, but I'll be taking whatever's left of my vacation time, so I'll clean out my desk now."

"Wait, Callie, let's not be rash," he called, chasing me down the hall.

"The only rash around here is the one on your lips from kissing the district attorney's ass."

With my assistant's help, I cleaned out my office and then headed to my car, my phone ringing just as I climbed in.

"This is Callie."

"Hi, Callie. This is Dr. Gardner."

I bit my lip. "Ah, hi. Thanks for calling me back. I'm not really sure what to say, to be honest."

"How about I save you the grief?" she asked. "You called while I was in with Pea, so I asked him if I could tell you anything."

I pressed my hand to my stomach. "And?"

"He said I could answer any questions you have."

"Is he...?" I swallowed. "Is he okay?"

"Well, that's relative," she said. "He's alive, which had it been someone smaller and not in as good of shape as him, wouldn't be the case."

I bit my fist and tried not to cry out in anguish. "Okay. Um...does he need anything?"

"No, he's being taken care of. Physically, anyway."

"Right. Of course he is. Well, I appreciate you calling me. Please send him my best wishes for a speedy recovery."

"Callie?"

"Hm?"

"I'm going to say something, but if you repeat it, I'll deny every word."

I sniffed, tears streaming down my face. "Okay."

"That boy is miserable, and not just from his physical injuries. I don't know what happened between the two of you, and it's none of my business, but if you feel about him the way I think you do, let it be known."

"Right."

"But let me also say, that if this isn't what I think it is, and you don't have deep feelings... ones that make you ready to fight with and for him, then you need to walk away and never look back. It's going to take months, possibly years for him to heal, and it's going to take hard work and someone who won't kowtow to him or get frightened away. By him or anyone else."

I was in full sob mode now but trying so hard to hide it. "Can he walk?" I rasped.

"Not right now. He does not have a spinal injury,

though, so once his legs heal, he will."

"Okay. That's good. Right? That's good?"

"Yes, that's hopeful," she said. "But PT's going to be a bitch for him...and for anyone in his sphere of influence."

I nodded, unable to form words, let alone sentences.

"He's at OHSU, currently in ICU."

"Can...can I see him?"

"Only you can answer that, Callie. Do you have permission? Yes. But, I'm serious, if you come, you're in."

"I understand."

"Okay. I'll let you go. I won't tell Pea about our conversation until you make a decision."

"I appreciate that, Dr. Gardner."

"Eldie, please. If Sweet Pea cares about you then you're family."

"Do you think he does? Care about me, I mean?"

"You'll have to find out for yourself."

She hung up and I spent the next fifteen minutes sobbing my eyes out in the underground parking lot of my office building.

Once I felt like I could drive in a straight line, I headed home.

I had some decisions to make.

* * *

Sweet Pea

I couldn't stop a groan as pain shot through my thigh and I came awake forgetting where I was for a brief second. Fuck me, everything still hurt like a mother fucker.

"Pea?"

The familiar voice covered me like a warm blanket,

but I couldn't really believe she was here, so I closed my eyes and tried to go back to sleep, assuming I was dreaming.

"Nurse? He's groaning in his sleep. He needs pain meds."

Okay, wait, that was definitely her voice. I took a chance and opened my eyes to see her leaning out of the door, demanding a nurse come and help me.

"Callie?" I rasped.

She turned and rushed back to the bed. "Hey. How much pain are you in? Someone's coming, okay?"

I reached for her hand, trying to keep her from disappearing. "What are you doing here?"

"First, do you want me here?"

I studied her. Jesus, she looked gorgeous. Her long blonde hair was pulled into a bun and piled on top of her head and she wore jeans that appeared to be painted on, along with a tight T-shirt that I wanted to peel off her.

"No," I said.

"Because?"

"You need to go, Callie."

She leaned closer. "You're an idiot, you know? I just want to make that fact clear."

"Call—"

"No," she said, interrupting me, sitting on the edge of the mattress and setting her hands on either side of my head, meeting my eyes. "You only want me to go because you're afraid."

"Doozer is dead."

"I know. Minus told me everything."

"Then you know the same people that tried to take me out, got to him, and I wasn't there to stop them. I can't let that happen to you. I care about you too much."

"I love you," Callie said, speaking the words I didn't have the courage to say. "So, this is how it's going to go. I'm here. Whether you like it or not, but only if you love me. If you don't, tell me now, so I can move on. But don't lie to me. I'll know."

And she fucking would. Jesus, she was perfect.

"Ten seconds, Pea," she warned.

"I don't want you saddled with this shit. Didn't you hear me about Doozer?"

"Yes, and I also heard you when you told me you wanted out of this life. And Minus when he told me that your club was trying to end this war."

I stared, stunned by what I was hearing.

"I told you, Minus told me *everything*."

"I'm hooked up to a piss bag, Callie."

"Congratulations," she said. "At least it's not a feeding tube because you're a vegetable and unable to feed yourself."

"I can't be the man you need."

"Who the fuck are you to tell me what I need? I'm quite capable of taking care of that myself," she said. "And let's be honest. I really just need your mouth and your dick. The rest is simply a minor bonus."

I bit back a laugh and stared at the woman who had my heart, my head, my entire being.

"You love me," she said, and tried to stand, but I grabbed her arms.

"Yeah, Callie, I love you, but that's not enough."

"It's not enough if you're not willing to fight, you're right. But I'm here, you're here, and I'm a fucking warrior. Are you?"

"Call—"

"I asked you a question, Pea. Are you a fucking warrior?"

"Fuck yes."

She smiled, leaning down to kiss me. "I'm glad to see you've pulled your head out of your ass."

I chuckled, my body screaming in pain with the action.

"Shit. Sorry, honey," she whispered. "Where the hell is that nurse?"

"Wait," I said. "I want to make sure you're really here before they drug me up again."

"I don't know if I'm brave enough to suck you off right here, right now, but I could try giving you a handy under the sheets," she said.

"I swear to Christ, woman, you need to stop making me laugh... and hard."

She bit her lip, leaning down to kiss me again. "Sorry, not sorry."

"Did Minus really talk to you about the club?"

"Yes, but he hired me as his lawyer first, so everything he said is protected by attorney client privilege."

"God damn, you're smart."

"And, you need sleep," she said.

"I love you," I whispered.

"I know," she whispered back, but before she could kiss me again, my nurse walked in and gave me a dose of pain meds, and I fell asleep with a smile on my face for the first time since this nightmare started.

FIFTEEN

BURNING SAINTS

Sweet Pea

AN INTENSE WARM sensation washed over me as a familiar voice spoke my name. I wasn't fully awake, but I didn't feel like I was dreaming.

"Sweet Pea. Don't worry. Everything's gonna be alright," Doozer said, and I opened my eyes to see him standing over my bed, dressed in white. He was smiling wide and I swear I could feel his touch when he took my hand. The moment he touched me, I felt an overwhelming peace and the urge to sleep pulled me deeper and deeper into the blue, until there was only black.

* * *

I was startled awake by the sound of movement in my

room.

"Wake up, baby brother," Ropes said in a tone far too cheery for whatever the fuck time it was.

"What the hell?" I groaned, my head swimming. "What time is it?"

"It's early. We had to sneak in during the middle of the night. We've been here for a while, but you were pretty out of it when we arrived, so we let you sleep," he said.

"We?" I asked, picking up my only friend, the morphine button, but Ropes stopped me. "Hold on there, bro."

I was disoriented and unaware of how long I'd been asleep or when my last dose was.

"I need my meds, Ropes," I protested. I was annoyed enough that he'd woken me up, and now he was really pissing on my picnic. However, before I could argue further, I noticed Minus standing at the foot of my bed with Trouble and seeing her was ten times better than any dose I could have received. She ran to me, threw her arms around me and began to cry.

"I'm so sorry," she sobbed.

"Hey, you have nothing to be sorry about. I'm just glad you're okay."

"If I had never left the Sanctuary you wouldn't have come after me and this wouldn't have happened."

"None of that matters. The only thing that's important is that you are alive," I said.

"That they are both alive," Ropes said, and I looked to see Doozer standing next to him. Instinctively, my body jolted, causing pain to shoot through my ribcage, but I barely cared.

"Holy shit," I exclaimed. "What…what the hell? How the fuck are you alive, kid?"

At that moment, I realized that I wasn't hallucinating

from the meds or receiving a visitation from Doozer's ghost. He was alive and standing right next to my bed.

"Shhhhh," Doozer hushed me with a smile. "Keep it down, will ya?"

"What the fuck is going on here?"

"It's me, Pea. I'm okay," Doozer said, putting his hand on my shoulder.

"I don't understand," I said, my head racing a hundred miles an hour. "We thought the Spiders got to you. They sent us your kutte, with…"

"Maybe I should explain," a doctor that was standing with Minus said. He was dressed in surgical scrubs, looked to be in his early thirties with a scruffy beard, and longish brown hair that was clumsily tucked into a surgical cap.

"Somebody better had, Doc," I said, to which he laughed.

"I'm not a doctor," he said, and it wasn't until then I noticed that Doozer was wearing a physician's lab coat, thus him being dressed in all white in my "vision."

"Wait a minute, what the fuck is going on here? Why are you guys dressed like that?"

"We had to sneak them in, disguised as doctors in case the Spiders have eyes on the hospital," Minus said.

"My name is Agent Rand Davis with the F.B.I."

"The fuck you are," I replied.

"I've been working undercover as a member of the Gresham Spiders for the past six months."

"Now I know for sure that I'm high as a fucking kite."

"I can assure you my credentials are real, as is this case," he said, producing an F.B.I. shield and I.D. "What's also real, is that as a member of the Spiders, I was ordered by Wolf to kill Doozer."

I looked at him puzzled.

"And deliver his heart to you," he said.

"Good thing he did, too," Doozer said. "If Wolf had given the job to another Spider, that would have been my actual heart inside that kutte."

"Whose fuckin' heart was it?" I asked.

"My office procured a substitute heart from the city morgue," Agent Davis said.

"And Wolf bought that?" I asked.

"Didn't you?" he retorted. "Doozer here was quite cooperative in posing for phony execution pictures. Post and during."

"It was fucking awesome, Pea," Doozer said excitedly. "We had all this fake blood and shit, and—"

"Let's save that story for later," Minus said.

"If you've only been with the club for six months, why the hell did Wolf give the job to you?" I asked.

"To prove my loyalty to the club. My way of earning my patch. Plus, he trusts me."

"Why's that?"

"I served in the middle east with Trunk, the Spiders V.P. We were Rangers together. When we got out, I went to Quantico and Trunk went sour."

"And when the Fed brass found out that you had an in with the Spiders via your connection with Trunk—"

"They didn't have to find out anything. I let my superior know about the possible connection as soon as I found out about Trunk's involvement with the Spiders. I'm working with an agent who's done covert work with MCs before. He was able to help me create a solid backstory about where I've been since leaving the army, as well as plant a few street-cred breadcrumbs for me."

"Cutting your heart out will be the nicest thing Wolf does to you if he finds out you're a fed," I said.

"I'm hoping with your help, that won't happen, and that we can put Wolf away in a Federal penitentiary for the rest of his life."

"My help? Why the fuck would I help the Feds?"

"Because Wolf is asking for a sit down with you," Minus said.

"What?"

"He knows you survived the crash and put the word out that he's willing to negotiate if you're delivered to him," Minus said.

"You think he really wants to talk about a truce?" I asked.

"I think if you go to that meeting, you don't come out alive," Minus said.

"So, what's the plan?" I asked.

"Our plan is to give him what he wants," Agent Davis said. "Or at least, make him think we have. This sit down presents us with a unique opportunity to gain information we've so far been unable to."

"What makes you think I can get him to talk?"

"You and Wolf have history. The way Minus tells it, it sounds like he was a mentor to you, and from what I've seen, Wolf has a real hard on for you."

"Gee, really? What tipped you off, the tire tracks across my face?" I asked.

"We only need to get you in a room long enough to record him admitting to Char's murder. Once we have that, we can safely extract you and arrest Wolf."

"And what if Wolf does try to kill me during the meeting?"

"We're working on making sure that doesn't happen," Agent Davis replied.

"Now that I've heard your plan, I think you're the one who's high on pain meds," I replied.

"Excuse me?" Agent Davis asked. "I would have thought you'd be the first to want Wolf dealt with."

"First, I'm not a fucking narc. Second, you could

have gotten a lot of people killed with that heart stunt of yours. I'm in this hospital bed thanks in part to you, and I'm supposed to just put my life in your hands so you can get a recording?"

"After months of risking my life, I'd put myself in the perfect position for Wolf to give me the job. When he gave me the order I had to answer quickly and decisively. If I'd hesitated, he would have sniffed me out and Doozer and Trouble would both be worm food. It was the best play I had, and I chose to roll the dice."

"You rolled the dice with our lives, Agent Dickface. We were ready to go to war with the Spiders over Doozer."

"You're already at war and Wolf wants every Saint dead," Agent Davis said.

"This guy saved my life, Pea," Doozer said.

"And mine," Trouble added.

"Look, Agent—"

"Call me Taxi, it's easier for me to keep my cover straight."

"Even if I wanted to, do I look like I'm in any kind of condition to help anyone? I can't even wipe my own fuckin' ass. You can keep your little plan to yourself. I don't need to hear anymore," I said. "Besides, how do I know the Feds aren't gonna come after us as soon as you're done with the Spiders?"

"Let me assure you the F.B.I. isn't interested in your club. We know since Frank Cutter's death, the Burning Saints have been pursuing legitimate business avenues. We also know that Wolf's split from the Saints was a result of the club's direction change. Our investigation is solely focused on the criminal activities of the Gresham Spiders."

"The federal prosecutor is willing to grant you full federal immunity of all past crimes in exchange for your cooperation in this investigation," Taxi said.

"And if I say no?"

"Then we won't be able to protect you should your war with the Spiders put your club in the crosshairs of our investigation."

"Meaning, the Feds don't give a shit about us now, but if I don't cooperate, they're gonna start caring," I said.

"Let's just say it's in everyone's best interest if you assist us in this investigation."

"I'm not wearing a fucking wire," I said.

"We don't want you to. Just hear me out for a minute and then you can make your decision," Taxi said. "Wolf wants a sit down with you, so we're going to give it to him. He'll probably search you when you arrive, so traditional listening devices are out, and we don't know where the meeting will take place, so we can't rely on a shotgun mic, but the bureau has a new recording device that's nearly undetectable that we want to use. It's super thin, completely shielded and since it's a recorder and not a transmitter, doesn't emit detectable radio frequencies."

"Pretend I'm not in the spy game," I said. "What the fuck does all that mean?"

"It means we'd send you into the meeting with an undetectable recorder sewn into one of the patches on your kutte. You get Wolf to admit to Char's murder, the F.B.I. gets our man, and you get immunity for any and all past crimes."

"No," I said.

"What?"

"No," I repeated. "It's not enough. I want full immunity for the whole club. All past sins forgiven. What any of us does from here on out we've gotta pay for like everyone else, but as far as the Feds are concerned, the

163

Burning Saints are as pure as the driven fuckin' snow starting now."

"I can't authorize that."

"Then you can get the fuck out of here. Before you go, be sure to leave a mailing address, so I can send your stunt heart back to you."

"You have to be reasonable," Taxi said.

"Reasonable? You want to use me as bait to get the guy who just tried to kill me, and is probably gonna try again, and you want to nickel and dime me?"

"Okay, I'll tell my boss your terms first thing in the morning and he can talk it over with the prosecutor, but I can't make any promises."

"Fair enough."

"And if they agree?" Taxi asked.

"Tell me what I need to do, and I'll do it."

SIXTEEN

BURNING SAINTS

Callie

"**D**ON'T SIGN ANYTHING until I look it over," I ordered Sweet Pea as he thumbed through the F.B.I.'s offer.

"I think I can handle reading, baby. My eyes aren't broken."

"No, but I have more experience with legal documents, and I want to make sure the F.B.I. doesn't try to screw you via a loophole. Will you let me look it over first, please?"

Sweet Pea smiled, handing the agreement to me.

I kissed him gently. "Thanks. Maybe reading this will help keep my mind off what you're about to do."

"Taxi will have me covered," Sweet Pea said, trying unsuccessfully to reassure me. "If Wolf agrees to the meeting, that is."

"I hope he doesn't."

"Callie, what I'm about to do is gonna wipe the slate clean for the club."

"But why does it have to be you?"

He raised an eyebrow. "I warned you, counselor. My life is crazy."

"Crazy doesn't scare me, but losing you does."

"I promise I'll be back. I'm not going to walk out on you."

"You *can't* walk."

Sweet Pea smiled, "I'll make sure they wheel me back to you in one piece."

"I hate this plan," I said.

"I love you," Sweet Pea replied.

"Dropping the L bomb isn't fighting fair," I said, as my insides turned to goo.

* * *

Sweet Pea

Minus's phone buzzed.

"Unknown number. This has got to be him," he said, holding the phone up.

"Okay, showtime," Agent Jaxon Quinn said, quieting the room.

Minus answered and put the call on speakerphone.

"This is Minus."

"You been getting my messages?" Wolf asked.

"I heard you wanted to talk, so let's talk." Minus said.

"We alone?"

Minus wasn't about to tell him about the team of

F.B.I. agents in the room listening to the call, or the one currently embedded in his club but didn't want to seem suspicious either.

"No," he replied. "Clutch is here with me.

"That's basic human anatomy, isn't it?" Wolf asked. "The asshole is always near the pussy."

"What do you want, Wolf?"

"Same as you, Minus. Peace," Wolf said, in a syrupy sweet tone.

Just hearing Wolf pretend to want peace made my flesh crawl. We didn't know what he was up to, but a peace summit it most certainly was not.

"You'll have to forgive me if I have a hard time believing that," Minus replied.

"My dear Minus, any recent tragedies your club may have suffered have nothing to do with me." Wolf poured on the fake legalese.

Taxi was right. Wolf was careful not to incriminate himself. He may have been a psychopath, but he was smart enough to know someone could always be listening. It's what made me so nervous about the FBI's plan. On the other hand, it's also what made the plan, and my involvement necessary in the first place.

"I don't care about any of that now, I just want for our clubs to make peace and negotiate terms we can both live with."

"I'm glad to hear that, Minus, but I'm nervous you won't be willing to do what it takes to make me feel comfortable with having a sit down."

"Set the terms," Minus said coolly.

"Only our mutual friend could settle this thing between us, but I hear he had a bad wreck and is in the hospital," Wolf said.

"I could make that happen," Minus said. "It might take a couple of days to arrange transportation, but I'll do it if it means peace."

"If you can get our friend to a meeting place, I'll talk to him. Alone," Wolf said.

"I think you and I need to speak, don't you?"

"No. I want to see our friend, alone. If I like what he has to say, then you and I can meet. Those are my terms. Take 'em or leave 'em, farm boy."

"Time and place."

"Tomorrow night, 10:00 P.M. at Cliff's old place. You know the spot I'm talking about?"

"I know it," Minus replied, looking at Agent Quinn, who was signaling for him to keep going.

"If I show up and catch one whiff of shit on anyone's shoe within a five-mile radius, it's all over. You understand?"

"You're calling the shots," Minus said.

"Don't fucking forget that," he said and hung up.

"Excellent work," Special Agent Jaxon Quinn said.

Special Agent Jaxon Quinn was the lead agent on the current investigation of the Gresham Spiders MC, and Taxi's handler. In another twist of fate, he happened to be related to two of the Dogs of Fire members, not to mention, he'd worked with the club on a previous investigation into human trafficking. I liked him and the Dogs vouched for him, so as far as I was concerned, so long as we got our immunity deal, my job was to say yes to whatever Agent Quinn said.

Taxi had approached Minus with the FBI's plan the morning after I was hit. He told Minus all about his undercover operation, and that he'd devised a plan after spotting Trouble while on night patrol at the Spiders' clubhouse.

Trouble was posted on the ridge overlooking the clubhouse armed with her father's sniper rifle. Her plan was to take out Wolf with an almost two-hundred-yard shot and then beat it out on foot. She'd taken an Uber most of the way and ran the last half-mile before making her way to the location where he'd found her. Since none of the other Spiders had seen them, he was able to take her safely to the motel where he'd stashed Doozer, whom he'd also saved. It goes without saying that Minus and the Saints were extremely grateful to Taxi for what he'd done for Trouble and Doozer.

"I don't like this," Minus said the moment he hung up.

"Tell me about the location," Jaxon said, ignoring Minus's protest.

"It doesn't matter, because I'm not leaving Sweet Pea there alone," Minus dug in.

"Every plan requires a bit of improvisation."

"Improvisation? We're not putting on a fucking summer camp talent show skit, Jaxon."

Jaxon sighed. "We were always going to have to fill in certain details as we went along. You knew that, Minus."

"Not this detail," Minus snapped. "You were certain Wolf would want to meet in a public place. Somewhere you could post undercover agents. The spot where Wolf wants to meet is out in the open and secluded."

"Look, Minus. I've been clear about this from the beginning. We need Wolf to confess to organizing the hit on Char. It's the final piece of damning evidence my boss needs to complete our investigation against the Spiders. We've got enough for indictments, but his confession would not only seal the Spiders' fate but make my boss's career. Plus, between you and me this is personal on our end almost as much as it is on yours."

"Why's that?" Minus asked.

"Two reasons. One, Char had cut a deal and was going to cooperate with the F.B.I., but Wolf got to him first."

"No fucking way," Minus said. "Char was evil, but he was an OG and would never turn on his own club."

"Char was a scared old man that was facing down spending the rest of his life rotting away in a maximum-security prison. Believe me, he would have traded his own mother for the deal we made with him."

"But Wolf got to him first, huh?" Minus asked.

"Our case took a big hit when we lost Char as an informant and my boss wants Wolf to hang for it. The other reason is more personal. Agent Davis wasn't the first undercover operative to infiltrate the Spiders. Another agent had already successfully infiltrated their ranks, but Wolf murdered him, along with two other Spiders during his recent hostile takeover. My Boss wants Wolf to fry and it's my job to make it happen by whatever means I have available to me."

"I'll do it," I said from my state-of-the-art wheelchair. "I'm cool with whatever Wolf wants to do. If Taxi says he'll have my back if I get into trouble, then I'm good."

"You shut the fuck up, Hot Wheels. You don't get a vote," Minus said.

"The hell I don't! It's gonna be my busted-up ass dangling out there on that hook," I argued.

"It was never part of the plan for him to be that exposed," Minus shouted at Jaxon.

"Do you trust your guy?" Jaxon asked Minus, motioning to me.

"Of course," Minus said.

"I trust my guy, too, and if Davis says he'll have Sweet Pea's back, I believe him. Besides, you know as well as I do, we have to make Wolf believe he has all the power."

Minus ran his hand down his face before turning to

me. "I guess it's your call."

"Then I say we do what Wolf says and trust that Taxi's as good as he says he is," I replied.

"I don't want to be in a position where we have to find out," Minus said.

"Then we are on the same page," Jaxon said, extending a hand to Minus, which he shook.

"Just so we're clear though," Minus said, pulling Jaxon closer. "He comes back any more fucked up than he already is, I'm likely to violate that immunity deal pretty quickly."

"This is going to work."

"It better," Minus said.

* * *

Taxi

Wolf hung up, put his phone in his kutte pocket, and slowly looked around the room to each of us. Present were Trunk, Flash, Slammer, who had now recovered enough from his knife injuries to ride, as well as veterans, Vega and Carver.

"The young lion has shown his throat even sooner than expected," Wolf said as he paced the room.

"Your plan worked, then?" Trunk asked, with a smile.

"Maybe too well," Wolf said slowly, as if working out a problem in his head.

"What do you mean? What did Minus say?"

"He's agreed to the meeting between me and Sweet Pea."

"Isn't that what you wanted?"

"He says he wants peace and he's willing to do whatever it takes, but I'm not buying it. He's up to something. I just don't know what."

I concentrated on my breathing and reminded myself that Wolf's suspicious nature would play to our advantage. In fact, we were counting on it.

"So, what's the plan?" Trunk asked.

"I gave Minus the time and location. If he shows up with the cripple and hands him over to me without any issues, I'll hear him out," Wolf said.

"Really?"

"Yeah, right after I put a bullet through Sweet Pea's neck."

I steadied my nerves and made sure not to react.

Wolf continued, "I told Minus, if I liked what I heard from Sweet Pea, I'd consider their surrender, but all I want to hear from Sweet Pea is the gurgling in his throat as he chokes to death on his own blood."

"And you really think Minus is just going to hand his lamb over for you to slaughter?" Trunk asked.

"I'm not going to give him a choice," Wolf said with a sneer.

Callie

"**G**OOD MORNING, YOU two," Katie Jameson said as she waltzed into Sweet Pea's room. "How's my favorite patient?"

Sweet Pea grinned. "Ready for my sponge bath."

I groaned. "*I* will be handling your sponge baths, jackass."

"That's what I meant," he said, and Katie chuckled. "Did you know that Katie's brother's a Dog?"

I frowned. "Like he identifies as a dog?"

Katie laughed. "No, the Dogs of Fire MC."

"*Oh,*" I said, feeling the heat creep up my neck.

"Don't tease her," Katie admonished, taking Sweet

Pea's vitals. "Besides. You never know these days. Keep Portland weird, right?"

"Don't worry about Callie. She loves being teased," he countered.

"The jury's still out on that," I grumbled.

"You'll have to come to a family night," Katie said. "Both of you. Well, unless, you just want to come, Callie."

"She's not goin' to a club party without me," Sweet Pea growled, and Katie gave me a wink.

"Don't tease him," I said.

"But he likes to be teased," Katie joked.

My stomach growled and Sweet Pea raised an eyebrow. "Baby, go get food."

"I don't want to leave you."

"I'm going to be here for a bit," Katie said. "You've got time."

I nodded and headed to the cafeteria, grabbing a few 'illegal' things for Pea as well. As I walked back toward Sweet Pea's room, I saw Katie talking with someone I recognized really well. "Oh my god, Grace?" I asked.

Grace Lundy's face lit up and she held her arms out. "Callie? What are you doing here?"

"My...I don't really know what to call him...man's here."

"Wait, you're with Sweet Pea?"

I nodded. "Yes. How did you know?"

"Flea's my husband," she explained. "Katie's brother. I'm here to take her to lunch, actually. Our whole club's been on high alert since everything that's happened. I'm so glad Sweet Pea's going to be okay."

I sighed. "Me too. I can't believe we've run into each other like this. I was just talking about you."

"About me?"

"Well, about a sleep over we both went to at Taylor

Beeman's house."

"Over spring break in eighth grade," Grace said.

"Yes! I can't believe you remember."

"How could I forget? I was traumatized and you were the only one who didn't make fun of me. I remember you let me hide with you in your sleeping bag while we watched scary movies."

"*Lost Boys*," I said.

"I still can't eat rice to this day," Grace said.

"Shut up," I shouted a little too loud for a hospital hallway. "I thought I was the only one. Sweet Pea even called me crazy. Do you want to come say hi?"

"Only if he's okay with it," Grace said.

"Give me a second," I said, and walked into Sweet Pea's room.

"Hey, baby," he said.

"Hey. You're never going to guess who I just ran into."

He cocked his head. "Who?"

"Remember how I told you I watched *The Lost Boys* at a slumber party?"

"Ah, yeah."

"Well, Grace was at that same party, and guess who she is?"

"Who?"

"Flea's wife."

"Oh, shit. I know Grace. She's cool as fuck."

I nodded. "I know. She wants to say hi, if you feel up to it."

"Tell her to get in here."

I set my food on the table and then called Grace in.

She walked in and gently hugged my man, then leaned against his bed. "You freaked us the fuck out, Sweet Pea. I almost hid the keys to Flea's bike."

"I know, babe, sorry."

"Gracie, if we're gonna go, we should go now." Katie peeked her head into the room. "Otherwise, I'll never get out of here."

"Okay," Grace said. "I'm taking her to lunch, and she's mean when she's hungry."

I chuckled, hugging Grace, and then once she left, I closed the door, opened the food bag and set all manner of surprisingly delicious food on the table.

"What did you bring me?" Sweet Pea asked.

"Breakfast burrito with extra bacon."

"And this is why I love you."

I grinned, pulling his tray over him. "Yeah, yeah, I know. You feel ready for tonight?"

"Nope."

"Well, don't try to sugar coat it on my account." I laughed nervously.

"Normally, I wouldn't give a second thought to going toe-to-toe with Wolf. Don't get me wrong. He is a dangerous psychopath who could easily kill me—"

"Again, no need for flowery speech to spare my feelings."

"You said you were one hundred percent in, remember?"

"You're right, and I am, but I'm still freaked out, and knowing you're afraid makes me want to freak out even more."

"I'm not afraid, Callie. It's worse than that. I feel helpless."

I'd never seen Sweet Pea look so vulnerable before and couldn't imagine ever loving him more than I did at that moment. I was also more terrified than I'd ever been.

"It's my first sit down, and literally all I can do is *sit down*."

"What exactly is a sit down?" I asked.

"Basically, it's a meeting where two bikers can hash their shit out without the fear of getting shot to death."

"Well, that sounds promising," I said.

"Normally I'd agree with you, but Wolf and the code aren't exactly best friends."

"The code?"

"Outlaw bikers are… funny," Sweet Pea said, with a chuckle void of humor.

"What do you mean?" I asked.

"They spend their lives avoiding the rules and regulations of 'the Man' only to live under a self-imposed biker code of conduct, which has its own set of rules and regulations," he replied.

"I assume the two rulebooks are quite different."

"Sure. Break the Man's law and you end up in jail. Break the code and you end up in a hole in the desert."

"At whose hand?"

"Motorcycle clubs can only co-exist in an area if a certain level of cooperation happens between them. If one club or member continually steps over the line, other clubs will band together and deal with it. Sit downs are sacred and to spill blood at one, tends to bring hell from other clubs. War is bad for business and nobody wants to be on the cops' radar, so most clubs fall in line…more or less."

"So why does Wolf want war so badly?"

"I don't think he does. This is personal for Wolf. It was Char's vision to expand the Gresham Spiders' territory into Portland, and then up into Washington. For him it was a business decision, and he didn't expect any resistance from us."

"Because you'd just turned the Saints' protection business over to Los Psychos," I said.

"Look who's been paying attention in biker class," Sweet Pea said, motioning me to his lips. "Come get your gold star."

I kissed him and said, "This would all be a lot more fascinating if the man I loved wasn't right in the middle of it."

"For Wolf, this is personal. I think he's wanted to wear the president's patch since the first time he put on a kutte. Turning his back on Minus the way he did was his way of saying he was the true Alpha."

"And then you made him look like a bitch," I said.

"Oh, fuck baby, my ribs," Sweet Pea gasped for air in between shallow bursts of laughter.

"I'm so sorry, oh my God. I hate all of this."

"I'm sorry you have to go through this," he said.

"I know, and to be honest, it's not what's bothering me the most," I said.

"What is it, babe?"

"I feel stupid bringing it up with everything else that's going on."

"What is it? You can say anything."

"That's just it," I said. "I can say anything to you, but what about you to me?"

"I kept details about my club from you to protect you," Sweet Pea said.

"No, you kept them from me to protect you and your club, and I understand that. But you could have been honest with me from the start."

"How could I have known that?" Sweet Pea asked.

"Minus did," I replied.

"Wow, that's not fair," he said, clearly hurt.

"What's not fair is that Minus trusted me the second I asked him to tell me everything, but you couldn't."

"I don't know why Minus was willing to say word one to you about club business, but I've come to trust his methods even when I don't understand them. Which is most of the time."

"The point isn't about Minus, it's about you."

"What do you want me to say?"

I stood up and paced. "Say *anything* as long as it's open and honest. Tell me something that lets me know you're as invested in this relationship as I am. As soon as I heard about your accident, I left my job and came right here to the hospital."

"I know, baby."

"No, I mean I *left* my job, as in I quit."

"You're kidding."

"Gregg was giving me crap about taking a few personal days and I just sort of exploded on him. My need to be here with you made me do the thing I already knew I had to do. I heard your voice in my head telling me to bet on myself. My love for you helped make me brave. Do you understand?"

"I understand, I just wish it was as easy for me to be so open about certain shit."

"Easy? Do you think anything in my life has been easy since we met?" I asked.

"Then why stick around?"

"Because I fell in love with a person, not a sack full of circumstances," I replied. "I love you for the person I know you to be. Strong, yet gentle. Kind, yet protective. Controlled, but still takes risks. And most of all, driven by justice."

Tears filled Sweet Pea's eyes. "Callie, there are so many things that aren't on that list."

"I don't care."

"But you do care. You want me to talk about my past and open up about what I've gone through. Some shit was written on that list during that time of my life, and I've written my fair share since joining the club. You don't know how fucking damaged I am."

"And you're afraid of what? That I'd leave you if I

knew?"

"Yes!" Sweet Pea shouted, clutching his ribs.

I rushed to him, but he waved me off.

* * *

Sweet Pea

"I'm okay," I groaned as Callie approached the bed. I was in too much pain to be touched. My doctor had been weaning me off the pain meds over the past few days, as this would be my last night in the hospital. Hopefully, it wouldn't be my last night on earth, but I couldn't deny it was a possibility. If I did make it out of the sit down alive, I was going to spend the rest of my time at Eldie's clinic, where the club had setup a rehab suite for me.

After several moments of silence, Callie spoke, "Whatever happened in your past. Whatever you've done. It can't be worth carrying around like this, Pea," she said softly.

"My sins, I can live with," I said.

"It feels like you're living with everyone's sins on your shoulders," Callie said.

"Maybe I am," I growled. "My uncle's, my father's, my brother's. The list goes on if you really wanna fucking hear it."

"I do," Callie cried out, and I broke.

My body was too weak to hold in its secrets any longer, and my heart was too full of Callie's love to accept any more poison from my mind. For the first time in my life, the feeling I had throughout my body matched what I felt inside emotionally. I was broken in every way, and if this was going to be my last night on earth, I was going to use my brokenness to say the words I'd never had the strength to say before, to the only woman who'd ever loved me.

"My uncle raped me."

Callie said nothing. She just lowered the guard rail, climbed into the hospital bed and held me as I told her everything. I talked about the fucked up shit my uncle did, and how helpless and ashamed it made me feel. I told her all about how my father used his wealth and influence to cover the abuse up and the bloody way my brother dealt with it. I left nothing out, and Callie never flinched. If she had a question, she'd ask it, and I would answer honestly. It was the hardest thing I'd ever done and the closest I'd ever felt to another person.

Callie held me tight, and for the first time in as long as I could remember, I wept. More importantly, Charlie wept.

EIGHTEEN

BURNING SAINTS

Sweet Pea

WE ARRIVED AT the former location of the High Stepper Gentleman's Club at ten o'clock sharp to find Wolf and two other Spiders already there. Since sit downs were unarmed, it was tradition to bring lieutenants as backup just in case anything jumped off. So far, both sides appeared to be playing by the rules.

The "Stepper," as it was known back in the day, was run by a low-level gangster named Arnold "Cliff" Clifford, and was the hottest strip club in Portland. It also served as a neutral meeting ground for rival clubs to hash out disputes without spilling blood. At least it was until Red Dog, one of the founding Saints was beaten to death by a rival club in the parking lot. Our world began to change around that time and the new breed of bikers, like Wolf emerged.

The empty lot where the Stepper used to stand was located near the airport, next to the Red Letter Hotel, whose construction had been halted and abandoned in 2008. The huge lot was sparsely lit and completely exposed on all sides, except the one facing the hotel. It was a good strategic location with high visibility of incoming threats, which is precisely why it was used back in the day. Given its checkered past, I couldn't tell if Wolf choosing this location was a good or bad sign. Either way, I just wanted to get the feds what they needed and get the fuck out of here.

"You good?" Minus asked.

"A-fuckin'-okay," I replied

"Remember what Jaxon said. Stick to the script and use the signal if you feel unsafe," Minus said.

Since I wasn't wearing a wire, the F.B.I. would not be able to hear anything that was happening during the meeting. I had been instructed to give a hand signal as soon as I had Wolf's admission, and the team would come in to make the arrest. The problem was, the remote location Wolf chose meant the team had to park at a distance that would take them at least thirty seconds to reach us. This meant I had to give the signal without tipping off Wolf and hope the incoming arrest team didn't spook him or his goons. If Wolf caught wind of the operation, I'd only have Taxi to serve as my backup, and I had no idea if he'd be any help at all.

"What's to feel unsafe about?" I joked.

"I mean it, Pea. Give the signal if you feel like shit's goin' sideways. Even if you don't have the recording. You hear me?"

"None of this means shit unless the feds get what they want," I said.

"You ready?" Clutch asked.

I nodded and said, "Time to roll the bride down the aisle."

Minus and Clutch stepped out and opened the side door before the van's automatic wheelchair lift lowered me to the ground. I had just enough meds in me to keep from being in agony while still staying as lucid as possible. I was weak as fuck, and if Wolf were to make a move on me, there was little I could do about it. Tonight, I'd have to beat him with my brains instead of my fists, and hope the plan worked.

"Looks like the stories of your death may not have been that exaggerated after all," Wolf bellowed as we approached. "You look like a sack of shit."

"A one-ton sucker punch tends to do that to a person," I said.

"You'd know," Wolf snapped. "You're the sucker-punch expert."

"Is that what this is all about? Did I hurt your feelings when I hit you for betraying our club?"

"Is clocking me how you earned that?" Wolf asked, pointing to my Road Captain patch. "Your kutte goes great with that hospital gown by the way."

"You like it? I wore it just for you," I seethed.

Stick to the script, stupid. Don't let him rattle you.

"We're unarmed. I trust you are as well," Minus said.

"That would make you too trusting," Wolf said, and his two sidemen pulled their guns.

"What is this shit, Wolf?" Minus growled. "You know we still have the backing of Los Psychos and the other three clubs. We came here to talk peace. If you ice us, it'll be full scale war."

"Relax," Wolf said. "If I wanted you dead, you'd be dead already. I'm just making sure you can't sneak up on me like you did back at the clubhouse."

"This is fucked up," Clutch said.

"Trunk and Vega here are gonna search you and your van for weapons. Once I know you're clean, Road Rash and I can have our little chat," Wolf said, motioning to me. "But first, we've gotta make sure you haven't hidden anything in the wheelchair."

Trunk and Vega handed their pistols to Wolf, who pointed them at Clutch and Minus, before gabbing me by the arms and pulling me out of the chair. Searing pain shot down my spine and I groaned uncontrollably in helpless agony as they held me up.

"You motherfuckers!" Clutch yelled.

"Come on, Clutch. You can't really blame me for being cautious, can you?" Wolf asked, tucking one pistol in his waistband while keeping a bead on him and Minus with the other. With his free hand, Wolf examined the wheelchair before moving on to me. "You don't have any nasty surprises tucked anywhere in that gown, do you?"

Wolf began patting me down, pressing and poking any bandaged area he found along the way. The pain would have dropped me to my knees had Wolf's goons not been holding me up, and I cried out as he dug his thumb into my battered ribcage.

"I swear to God, Wolf, let him go or you're gonna regret it," Minus said, but Wolf paid him no mind, continuing his torturous frisk until I was almost unconscious from the pain.

Finally, Wolf said, "Okay, he's clean. Let him go," and the two did just that, allowing me to drop to the ground like a stone.

"Pea!" Minus shouted.

I lay on the ground in a crumpled heap as the two Spiders searched the van before returning to Wolf.

"It's clean," Trunk said.

"Alright, the two of you get him back into his chair and I'll wheel him over there," Wolf said, pointing to an unpaved area of the lot near a large walnut tree. "Then I want you two to take Midol and Crotch back to their cripple-mobile and keep an eye on them."

"What was all that bullshit about tossing your weapons?" Minus asked.

"You're an educated man, Minus. Who was that playwright that said that shit about "If you show a gun in the first act, you'd better use it in the second?"

"Was it suck my Longfellow?" Clutch said.

"Longfellow was a poet, not a playwright, but that was really good, buddy," Minus said.

"It would be a shame if a bullet broke up your little comedy act," Wolf said, before turning back to me. "Get him up," he barked, and I was put back into my chair with the same amount of care used when I was taken out if it.

Minus and Clutch were taken back to the van at gunpoint and Wolf wheeled me out to the spot near the tree.

"Maybe it's time for you and me to bury the hatchet. What do you think?" Wolf asked as we moved along.

The only place you'd put a hatchet is in my back.

"Ain't that what we're here for?" I asked.

"I don't know," Wolf said. "After all this time, I still can't quite figure you out."

"Was running me over some sort of half-assed attempt to study my brain?

"Come on, Sweet Pea," Wolf said bringing the chair to a stop once we reached the tree. "You've got me all wrong. I'm glad you're alive."

"Strange reaction from the guy who tried to kill me," I said, trying my hand at getting Wolf to incriminate himself.

"Who, me? I was home watching the fight," he said. "The article in the paper said it was a hit and run, isn't that right? Probably a drunk driver. You've gotta be careful out there, Sweet Pea."

Not only was his answer a bust, it made me want to beat the shit out of him even more.

"What about Doozer?" I asked, coughing up blood into my hand. "Did he slip in the fucking shower?"

"Now, Sweet Pea. Don't get all worked up. I thought you wanted to talk about peace."

Wolf wasn't making this easy, but rather than back down at all, I dug in.

"Minus said you'd talk about bringing this war to an end if I agreed to meet with you alone, so here I am. If you brought me here to kill me, I wish you'd make your move."

"I told Minus I'd talk to him if everything went well with us tonight. Plus, I told you I'm glad you're alive. In fact, I have a present for you."

Wolf reached behind the base of the tree and produced a burlap sack that looked both heavy and stained with blood.

"What the hell is this, Wolf?"

"Don't worry, Sweet Pea, it won't bite," he said dumping the contents of the sack in my lap; a large snake.

"Jesus, what the fuck!" I shouted, struggling to get the snake off me. It was only when it hit the ground that I could see the snake's head had been cut off.

"What's the matter? Not an animal lover?"

"You sick fuck," I said, regaining my composure. I studied the snake and a shock of panic hit me. "Where did you get this snake?"

"You know, it's the damnedest thing. Vega's little brother, Marco works at this little pet shop downtown. He cleans up cat turds and stocks shelves. You know, shit like that. But what little Marco wants to be when he grows up is a Spider, so he couldn't help notice when he saw a Burning Saints patch come into his store one night."

My fists clenched and my spine stiffened.

Wolf continued, "Marco said the Saint was buying feeder mice for his old lady's ball python, and Marco only knew of one hot chick with a ball python in the area."

I used every ounce of strength in my body to stand but was barely out of my seat when Wolf shoved me back down.

"I swear to God, if you touch her—"

"Can't say I've had the pleasure of meeting Callie Ames, Esquire, but maybe you can let her know I found her snake."

Fighting for the club or immunity was one thing, but now that I knew Callie was a direct target, I had to take Wolf out or die trying. This sonofabitch was gonna sing if I had to pull his voice box out and squeeze it like an accordion.

"So, that's your thing now. Going for the head? The snake, Minus, Char?"

"Char's celly did him. It's on the official report. I was at home watching the fight."

I forced a chuckle despite the pain. "I wouldn't try so hard to sell that story, some of your guys will actually believe you. Then you're fucked."

"What the hell are you talking about?"

"You took out your own club President and took his seat. The only reason you've been allowed to keep that seat is because your club fears you. If they really thought Char's cellmate killed him without your say so, then your Presidency is really thanks to some meth-head."

"Whatever," Wolf said, dismissively.

"Unless...oh, shit!" I said. "Char's celly really *did* kill him for his own reason's and you had nothing to do with it."

"What the fuck would it matter? Dead's dead and I was wearing the President's patch before Char bought it."

"Only because Char gave it to you temporarily while he was inside."

"What the fuck do you know?"

I shrugged. "Nothing, apparently. I thought you were behind Char's hit. I thought you'd at least earned your seat."

"Everything I got, I took with my own two hands. Just the way I like it. It's the whole reason I joined a club in the first place." He scowled. "Everyone knows, Cutter should have given me Red Dog's staff, but instead, he and Minus decided to turn the Burning Saints into some sort of sweatshop that knits pink pussy hats."

"So, it was easier to betray your club and take what belonged to another man, someone who had actually built his club from nothing? At least Char would have had the balls to kill his enemy himself."

"You know what, Pea? Because you and I have history, and because this conversation isn't gonna matter in thirty seconds, anyway, I'll be straight with you," Wolf said. "I did kill the old man. I took his club from him just like I'm gonna take the Saints from Minus. The only difference is, I'll get to stab Minus in the heart myself instead of having to hire a jailhouse rat to do it. Then when I'm done, I'm gonna introduce your lawyer girlfriend to my big ol' snake and you won't be around to stop me. You got anything cute to say about that?" Wolf asked triumphantly, as he pulled a .9mm pistol from inside his kutte.

"Yeah," I said, before raising my hand to give the signal. "Objection, mother fucker."

Before my hand reached the air, Wolf's gun, along with his right hand disappeared in a puff of pink mist.

Taxi's skills as a marksman were as good as advertised and his bullet found its target.

Wolf dropped to his knees, unable to utter a sound as he gripped his forearm, now gushing with blood.

I heard sirens approaching from the distance and sat silently as I watched Wolf convulse and bleed. I barely had time to process what happened when I heard Minus's voice call out, "Pea, you okay?"

"I'm good. Wolf is down," I replied, and he and Clutch ran to join me.

"Jesus Christ," Minus said, upon seeing Wolf, who was now attempting to "fix" his hand. Wolf frantically pulled at the few bits of skin and bone that hung from his bloody stump as arterial blood sprayed his face.

"I can fix this," Wolf said, clearly in a state of shock. "Help me find my fingers," he shouted as he began searching through the dirt.

Clutch kicked Wolf's gun out of reach and Minus checked on me.

"You okay?" he asked, and I nodded as federal agents swarmed the area.

Callie

"WHAT THE HELL happened?" I snapped as Sweet Pea was wheeled back to his hospital bed in Eldie's clinic.

"I'm okay," he rasped.

"You're *not* okay," I countered, as Minus and Clutch lifted him onto the mattress, and he groaned in pain. "You're hurt."

"It's fine, Callie," he said, but he looked far from it. His hospital gown was soaked in blood and he had fresh bruises on his arms and neck. He also looked dehydrated and exhausted.

Because Clutch was the closest to me, I turned on

him first, jabbing my finger into his chest. "You were supposed to have his back! You promised he'd be protected."

"Ow, babe, hold on," Clutch said.

"No, you fucking hold on," I growled. "How much more damage did you do to him? I swear to God, I will make you hurt if anything's permanent." I was screeching like a banshee now as I continued to jab at Clutch. If I'd been in my right mind, I might question why the big man just stood there and took it, but since I wasn't even close to sane at the moment, I continued to rail on him, "You promised me he'd be—"

"Jesus, Callie, enough!" Sweet Pea snapped.

"Oh, hell, no!" I turned to him. "You promised me you weren't going to be hurt! What did that monster do to you?"

A firm but gentle arm wrapped around my shoulders and I was pulled against Minus's granite like chest. "He's okay, sweetheart. It's all okay. We're gonna get some more pain meds in him, but he's okay."

I burst into tears, my anger evaporating into the terror I'd been dealing with all night, and I gripped Minus's kutte and sobbed into his shirt.

"Goddammit, Minus, release my woman," Sweet Pea demanded. "If you need to cry, you'll fuckin' do it with me."

"I don't want to hurt you."

"Get your ass over here," Sweet Pea said, and I climbed into the bed beside him.

He wrapped his arm around me and cradled me gently to his chest as Clutch and Minus left us alone.

"What did he do to you?" I rasped.

"It doesn't matter, baby. It's done. I'm here, I'm okay."

"Please tell me you ripped his dick off."

He chuckled, groaning at the obvious pain and I sat up. "Oh my god, honey, I'm sorry."

He tugged me back down and stroked my hair. "I'm okay, Callie. And Wolf's been dealt with."

"Sorry to interrupt," Eldie said, breezing into the room. "I need to get you checked out and give you some pain meds."

I moved to get up, but Sweet Pea held firm. "You'll need to do that with Callie right where she is."

Eldie smiled. "Okay, buddy, I'll do my best."

As Eldie did a quick wound check, I stayed put, but didn't fully relax until morphine was once again coursing through Sweet Pea's veins and the pain etched in the tight features of his face eased. He held me until he fell asleep and I would have stayed longer, but my bladder had decided it was time for me to move, so I did my thing, then tried to get comfortable in the chair.

A quiet moan from Sweet Pea had me up and at his bedside again. "Are you in pain?"

"Just my heart," he said melodramatically.

"Oh, lawd."

He reached for my hand. "Where'd you go?"

"To pee," I said.

"Get back in here."

"Are you sure?"

"I sleep better with you here, baby."

"Okay," I said, and climbed back onto the mattress.

Sweet Pea pulled me closer and I kissed him gently. "I love you, Pea. Thank you for not dying."

"Love you, too, baby." He kissed my temple. "And you're welcome."

"Do you need more meds?"

"No, I'm good. You make the pain go away."

"Oh my god, stop. What the hell is wrong with you?"

He chuckled. "Ow."

I reached for his pain pump button and pressed it.

"That's nice," he rasped, and I felt his body relax.

"Go to sleep, Pea," I ordered. "I'll be here when you wake up."

"Okay, baby."

Once I knew he was asleep, I allowed myself to fall into the abyss as well, and I did it with a relieved smile. There was nothing better than being curled up against my man where I knew he was safe and sound.

Callie

Two years later...

"HONEY, ARE YOU ready?" I called up the stairs.

Sweet Pea had studied his ass off for the Bar Examination, which he'd taken six weeks ago, and we were waiting to find out the results. They were supposed to be posted within the next thirty minutes, and Sweet Pea was a nervous wreck.

"No!" he bellowed.

I smiled. "You're gonna pass," I encouraged. "But we won't know until you log on."

"Why did I let you talk me into this?" he asked.

"I believe in you," I said, opening the door to Diamond and Sapphire's luxury enclosure, placing two feeders inside.

Directly after assisting the FBI, Sweet Pea moved me into his condo. Even though my place had a full-time doorman, he wanted me here, immediately. He even hired full-time security for the entire building. I soon found out that Sweet Pea's money wasn't at all connected to his family but came from real estate and business investments he and his brother had made.

As soon as he was released from Eldie's ad-hoc rehab clinic, Sweet Pea moved out of the Sanctuary and in here where the four of us have lived since. I say the four of us because Sweet Pea didn't come home alone. While still in rehab, he'd reached out to several reptile rescue organizations and was able to adopt two beautiful ball pythons which we named Diamond and Sapphire in memory of my sweet Ruby. The snakes were supposed to be a gift for me, but Sweet Pea called them his "lovely ladies" and pampered them as if they were our children. He custom built a home for them that took up an entire wall of the condo. I sometimes wondered if he loved those snakes even more than he loved me.

"Holy fucking fuckballs!" Sweet Pea shouted at the top of his lungs before appearing over the railing. "I passed the Bar," he said excitedly.

"You're a lawyer, baby," I said, smiling up at him, my heart bursting with pride.

"I'm gonna be a fucking lawyer!" he yelled as he barreled down the stairs before scooping me up into his arms and spinning me around.

"Careful, you're gonna make us throw up," I said and Sweet Pea set me down gently before giving me a kiss.

"You hear that little biker?" Pea said to my belly, "Your daddy's big time now."

"Charlie is not getting on a motorcycle. Ever," I said sternly.

"The hell she isn't," he said and grinned wide. "Besides, if she ever gets into a wreck, she can hire me as her lawyer."

"You plan on starting a practice specializing in personal injury?" I asked.

"Now that you mention it, it might be the right time for a career move. My boss is always hitting on me at work."

"Yeah? Well, I hear she'll soon be your partner because…"

"I'm gonna be a fucking lawyer!"

Sweet Pea and I celebrated into the wee hours of the morning. I hadn't stayed up that late since getting pregnant but didn't want to close my eyes for fear that I would miss out on a single moment. In the little over two years since Sweet Pea and I met, we'd managed to start a family law practice, an amateur reptile rescue sanctuary, and now, a family. I couldn't imagine being happier, especially knowing that Sweet Pea wasn't the only one that got to help put a monster behind bars.

My first client after opening the practice was Elsie Miller. We filed, and won, a civil suit against John Knight and she was awarded three million in damages. Knight was forced to liquidate his assets and the Miller family started a charitable foundation called Elsie's Riders that works together with our old friends Bikers for Kids. Together, they help kids to speak out against their abusers, and speak out, they did.

Elsie's story and her bravery inspired two more children to disclose abuse at Knight's hand and a new criminal trial was set. I was able to assist as special counsel under the new District Attorney, Rob Glass, and together, my old friend and I put Knight behind bars for two consecutive terms of ninety-nine years.

As I curled up against my man, my eyelids got heavier, and my thoughts turned to what our daughter might be like. I hoped she'd be tough like her auntie, Trouble, who had graduated top of her class at Quantico as a sharpshooter and was currently serving as an assistant trainer with her favorite professor and mentor, Agent Randall "Taxi" Davis. Sweet Pea and I couldn't be prouder of the amazing woman she'd become and were pretty fond of her guy, too.

Sleep came for me, but in the end, my life was far sweeter than anything I could have dreamed. I'd found my true calling, was about to have my first child, and most importantly, was sleeping next to the best chum I could have ever asked for.

A double shot of A.H. Hirsch Reserve 16-year-old straight bourbon whiskey in a glass (because Callie doesn't fuck around).

USA Today Bestselling Author Jack Davenport is a true romantic at heart, but he has a rebel's soul. His writing is passionate, energetic, and often fueled by his true life, fiery romance with author wife, Piper Davenport.

Twenty-five years as a professional musician lends a unique perspective into the world of rock stars, while his outlaw upbringing gives an authenticity to his MC series.

Like Jack's FB page and get to know him!
(www.facebook.com/jackdavenportauthor)

Made in the USA
Columbia, SC
03 February 2025